WIT

One star
from sudden
He was too busy staring up into slitted eyes of malevolent orange, a furrowed brow plate, two holes where a
nose should be, mashed, concave cheekbones, and a
slack, brutish mouth full of too many crooked teeth to fit
within it . . .

Not a single person on board the *Sabre* had a prayer of
survival.

OPERATION STARHAWKS

COMMANDER BRYAN KELLY. The Admiral's son whose
early mission ended in disaster. *Sabre* is his chance to redeem
himself . . .

DR. ANTOINETTE BEAULIEU. The brilliant but disillu-
sioned ship's medic, she's already been forced out of Spec.
Ops. once. She has a lot to prove.

CAESAR SAMMS. The only surviving member of Kelly's
first command. He's tough, loyal, and battle-hardened—but
his lack of caution can ruin them all . . .

PHILA MOHATSA. The volatile junior operative whose secret
past on a frontier planet has trained her in the use of
exotic—and illegal—killing tools . . .

OLAF SIGGERSON. An older, more experienced civilian
pilot, pressed into service, who rarely agrees with Commander
Kelly's judgment.

OPERATIVE 41. The genetically altered half-Salukan, dependable, but cold and impartial—who knows where his true
alliance lies?

OUOJI. The ship's mascot . . . and perhaps much more.

FULL SPEED AHEAD—
ADVENTURE AWAITS!

Ace Books by Sean Dalton

Operation StarHawks Series

SPACE HAWKS
CODE NAME PEREGRINE
BEYOND THE VOID
THE ROSTMA LURE
DESTINATION: MUTINY
THE SALUKAN GAMBIT

OPERATION STARHAWKS

BOOK SIX
THE SALUKAN GAMBIT

SEAN DALTON

ACE BOOKS, NEW YORK

This book is an Ace original edition,
and has never been previously published.

THE SALUKAN GAMBIT

An Ace Book / published by arrangement with
the author

PRINTING HISTORY
Ace edition / January 1992

ISBN: 0-441-63582-2

Ace Books are published by The Berkley Publishing Group,
200 Madison Avenue, New York, New York 10016.
The name "ACE" and the "A" logo
are trademarks belonging to Charter Communications, Inc.

PRINTED IN THE UNITED STATES OF AMERICA

10 9 8 7 6 5 4 3 2 1

PROLOGUE

Give revenge to the kinsman, for his aim is truest.

—Saluk proverb

Toiling in the darkest reaches of Mine 70 to load baskets of Tyrsian salt onto a motorized cart, Dausal bent over to pick up the last one when a whip cracked just centimeters above his head.

Instinctively Dausal dropped into a crouch, head bowed, arms hugging his knees. He shivered as much from fear as from chills. The infected shackle sore on his bare ankle stank with rot, and sweat poured off his half-naked body.

A light shone over him, blinding white. Dausal squinted, shrinking from it. The overseer loomed up and coiled his electric whip.

"You," he said, "are wanted in the warden's office. Make no move."

Dausal turned his face away from the light quickly to hide his expression. How long had it been since he'd last been hauled into the warden's office? A year ago? They'd told him then that his father was dead, as though he cared what became of the filthy traitor. Now what was the news? Had his accursed sister and her brood also died?

"Keyman," said the overseer.

The keyman, swathed in protective goggles and a dust filter, knelt beside Dausal with his tools. Dausal shifted away.

"No," he said in his ruined, hoarse voice. "Do not take me into the light. I do not want to hear words from the past."

The overseer struck hard with the lash, laying a sizzling cut across Dausal's shoulders. Crying out, he fell sprawling in the salty dust, his flesh burning like fire, his hatred consuming him. In that moment he hoped the overseer would kill him and end this wretched torment.

"Get up," said the overseer. He kicked Dausal in the abdomen. "Get up!"

Slowly, resentfully, Dausal righted himself. The overseer switched off the charge to his whip and hooked it about Dausal's neck, twisting it so that it became a noose.

"If the warden wants you, he will have you." The overseer yanked, and Dausal gasped for air. "If the warden wants to leave you in the sunlight until your eyes burst and your skin falls off your bones, it will be done." He yanked again. "You have no say in what is done and not done. You will be silent."

Dausal wheezed as the whip tightened around his throat. It pulled the protective cartilage of his neck against his air supply, choking him. The light within the tunnel wavered as his vision failed. He opened his mouth, but no air came in. His lungs began to labor, to panic. Just when he thought he would pass out, the overseer released him.

The sweet intake of air made Dausal cough. He leaned over, gasping raggedly. The keyman went to work quickly, freeing his shackle and chain from the ring bolt set in the stone floor.

"Up!" said the overseer.

Dausal braced his hands upon the wall and slowly maneuvered himself onto his feet. The overseer gave him a shove that nearly toppled him again.

"Move!"

Dausal had no choice but to obey.

The lift hauled him and the overseer straight up through the main shaft with a hydraulic whine that drowned out the echoing noises of the mine. At the top, the lift doors rolled open.

"Out!" said the overseer. He shoved Dausal hard enough to send him sprawling onto the platform.

Slowly Dausal managed to drag himself to his knees. The overseer kicked him high in the soft, vulnerable part of his chest. Dausal threw up blood. It tasted sour in his mouth. He wanted only to close his eyes and sink into permanent oblivion, but there was none.

One of the guards standing at the exit came over, the plaited ends of his wig swinging as he walked. "What is this?" he asked sharply. "Beating prisoners on the way up is against regulations."

The overseer grunted. "This one is a troublemaker. He has a deathwish."

"Did the warden send for him?"

"Ahe."

The guard gestured. "Get him out of here then. And make sure he is walking by the time he is outside. The warden has off-world visitors."

Dausal let himself feel a tiny sliver of hope. Perhaps his release had come at last. Then, as the overseer yanked him up and steered him toward the exit with a grasp like steel, Dausal angrily swept the hope aside.

Once he had been the brightest, most promising cadet within the 12th Lancers Corps, destined for a glorious career. But that was over. All he had left to live on was hatred. Hatred of his father Arnaht, who had sold out to the Alliance and defected to the Earthers, thus bringing shame upon all of them. Hatred of his sister, Melaethia, who had lain with Pharaon Nefir, then murdered him. Hatred of himself, who had done his duty and betrayed his father to the authorities.

Dausal's reward had been a sentence of life servitude. He could have been beheaded publicly as the son of a traitor. But because Nefir's death had opened the way for Raumses to seize the throne, Raumses had been lenient and spared him from execution.

This was a slower, harsher form of death. Even if they let him go, what was left of his dreams and ambitions except the burning desire for revenge? His father had already cheated him of that by dying. Would killing Melaethia be a sufficient substitution?

Outside, the harsh sunlight blinded him. He cringed, covering his face with his hands, but the light blazed against his shut eyelids until his eyes watered copiously. He had no more than one seared glimpse of a barren heap of discarded rubble, conveyor belts and loaders, heavy equipment, and corrugated porta-sheds, then he saw nothing else as the overseer steered him along to the warden's office.

There were few windows in the building, and after a few minutes Dausal's watering eyes adjusted. He found himself shoved into a concrete tank that smelled of chemicals. The overseer hosed him down with cleanser and disinfectant, leaving him dripping and battered from the harsh jets.

"Askanth, but you *still* stink," muttered the overseer. He threw a pair of shabby coveralls at Dausal, who before had been clothed in little more than ragged tatters.

Then, barefoot and still sniffing from the disinfectant that had been sprayed up his nostrils, Dausal limped down a long hallway that ended with a door flanked by two guards in tan imperial uniforms. Wigged, their faces decorated with paint lines, armed with short-range percussion rifles and ceremonial daggers reflecting their Houses and ancestry, they stood at perfect attention. They looked tireless, immovable, impassive. Their eyes stared right through Dausal as though he did not exist. The overseer gave the password, and one guard stepped aside.

Dausal shuffled by, ashamed by the surge of longing which filled his throat. He used to serve on guard duty. He had worn a medal of commendation upon his imperial sash. He might have been an oparch by now, if his life had not ended.

The door closed behind him, and a mirrored wall in the antechamber showed Dausal the reflection of an old man, stooped with crooked shoulders, dragging one leg, flesh covered with raw sores, a face worn down to skin and bone. Only his dark eyes remained recognizable.

Shocked, Dausal stared at himself. He had not yet reached his full majority of years, and yet he had become this monster. Tears welled in his eyes, then he blinked them back, running his tongue back and forth over his fangs to reawaken his fury.

He thought of his sleek, beautiful sister living upon Earther bounty and cursed her from the black pit of his soul.

The overseer shoved him. "The warden is ready for you. Go inside."

Some effort had been made to soften the crudeness of the warden's office with tapestry hangings and the luxuries of home. But the hangings were dusty, the brass lamps had become tarnished, and the aquarium stood empty, its sides stained white with dried mineral deposits.

The warden himself was absent, and a plainly dressed Salukan stood in his place by the desk. He turned as Dausal hobbled in, and his narrow face had the razor-fine features of a falt—proud flier of the southern highlands of Gamael. His skin had the pale golden cast of a southerner as well, and his eyes were the color of beer. Thin blue lines of his warrior status were drawn upon his cheeks, but he wore no other paint. His shaven skull was elongated and narrow. He possessed the air of command, but he wore no uniform. His clothing was instead simple coveralls of khaki, tailored and crisp, but plain of any decoration. In his hands he held a small jamming device to thwart any snoops planted in the room.

Dausal had not the least clue of who he was.

The stranger stared at Dausal for a full minute, neither speaking nor letting any expression enter his eyes.

Then he said, "The Pharaon is dead."

Dausal blinked, trying to comprehend words that had little meaning. "Dead," he said stupidly.

The stranger snorted and set the jammer upon the desk. "It took a great deal of trouble to find you. Try to reward that effort by pulling your wits together. I am Muetet ton Toth g Juvanne, head of the House of Toth."

Dausal's wits seemed lodged in glue. His own pain, the harsh light, the abrupt change in his surroundings, this abrupt stranger were too much to assimilate all at once. Through his muddled confusion, he grasped one fact.

"Toth," he said hoarsely. "My *masere*'s House."

"Yes, before her marriage your mother was of Toth."

Dausal lifted his gaze to Muetet's. "Have you come to release me or kill me?" he whispered.

A muscle tightened in Muetet's jaw. He said, "Raumses the Usurper is dead, leaving no heirs. Order is being restored even as we speak. It is in the interest of the House of Toth to reclaim you and your sister Melaethia."

Sister! Dausal tensed, longing to strike through her heart.

"She has borne Nefir heirs," said Muetet coldly.

Dausal gestured. "Demons! When she murdered Nefir she erased his name from her brats."

"Those children can inherit the throne which Raumses has left vacant," said Muetet.

The confusion cleared from Dausal's brain. With sudden clarity he understood it all. By putting one of Melaethia's brats upon the throne, the royal line was restored, yet power would be shifted into the hands of Toth and all its members. Nefir had been of the House of Juvanne, but because there had been no marriage between Nefir and Melaethia, her House had prior claim to the children.

Dausal clenched his battered hands into fists. "So still she wins," he hissed. "Damn her soul to the void—"

"Silence!" said Muetet sharply. "Curb your jealousy, fool, and listen further. As uncle to the new Pharaon, you stand to gain much from this."

"I want only her blood upon my hands," whispered Dausal.

"She is unimportant once all is in place," said Muetet. "But for now she is our path to power, and yours. Do you understand, or has your mind been broken in this place?"

Contempt dripped through his words, and for Dausal it was like a slap. What did it matter if he had been tortured and brutalized for two years? If such a fate befell a warrior, he was expected to endure it with honor.

Old feelings of pride came halfway to life within Dausal. He glared at Muetet. "And Arnaht, my father?"

"That name has been struck from memory," said Muetet. "As has been his House."

Dausal gasped. "All of them?"

"All."

Dausal turned away, struggling to comprehend that the entire minor House of Koult had been wiped out, thousands of its members executed. The blood must be running freely across the Empire.

"It was the doing of Raumses," said Muetet. "He butchered without compunction to secure his throne, but—"

"Who killed him?"

Muetet's eyes grew very cold, causing Dausal to regret the question as soon as it was uttered. "You need not suffer more for the sins of your father. Your father no longer exists, and you have been claimed by us. Do you accept that honor?"

Dausal wanted to weep, and his own weakness of emotion shamed him. He did his best to come to attention, although his stoop defeated him. "I accept it," he whispered hoarsely. "I wish to—"

He wanted to thank Muetet, to kneel at the man's feet and sob out his gratitude, but he knew better than to show such weak behavior.

"Good. You will be entered upon the rolls," said Muetet. "I have already arranged your release from this place. In a few minutes we'll be transported up to my ship where you will receive medical attention and a bath."

Dausal inclined. His sudden good fortune seemed too much to believe in, but if it was a dream he had no wish for it to end.

"Don't look at me as though I am Ru incarnate," said Muetet irritably. "I have read your records. You were an egotistical young fool stuffed with idealism and nauseating patriotism. I hope by now you've had that knocked from you."

Shame ran through Dausal like flames. He struggled to keep his temper under control. "I do not know," he said quietly.

"Then find out and take it from yourself," said Muetet, and his voice was as sharp as the overseer's whip. "You will do as you are told. You will not act on your own. We have many delicate maneuvers to achieve in reaching our ambitions. You are merely a tool. That must be clearly understood both now and later on."

Dausal bowed meekly, hiding his resentment. "I can take orders."

"You had better. Because you are going to find your sister and take her from the Earthers."

"I?" said Dausal in startlement. "Ah, no. That is not wise. I want to kill her. My blood has run hot these many months. It is all that has kept me alive. I am not the one for that task—"

Muetet struck him hard across the face, sending him reeling back. "You are precisely the one for the task," he said in a voice colder than space itself. "Because now that she has given herself into the keeping of the Earthers, the only one of us she will ever trust is you."

Pressing the back of his hand to his swollen mouth, Dausal muttered, "She knows I hate her."

"But she still loves you." Muetet smiled, but it was a chilling smile that did not reach his eyes. "There is much power in that. It will undo her as nothing else can."

"Why not just take the brats?"

"The Earthers guard them too well. No, Dausal. The only way we can succeed in regaining them is if we have your sister's cooperation. And that part of it is up to you."

1

Beware the sudden stranger at thy gate. His path is surely evil.
                                                        —ancient Salukan saying

Teleporting into the outskirts of Banqot meant materializing into a steam bath of heat and high humidity. Bryan Kelly blinked and sucked in a breath of hot, wet air. It was mid-day, and the weak sunshine trying to filter through a hazy cloud cover gave everything a faded, shimmery quality.

Overcoming his initial sense of disorientation, Kelly checked out his surroundings. They had been given teleportation coordinates on the outskirts of town in order to avoid alerting surveillance scanners. Kelly listened to a variety of creatures chattering and squawking in a small copse of nearby trees, the splash of running water behind a garden wall, and the muffled roar of traffic in the distance.

Satisfied, Kelly activated his comm. "Kelly to *Sabre*," he said. "Everything's fine. Send them down."

Seconds later, the blue and silver light of the teleport effect shimmered upon the deserted road, and 41 and Beaulieu materialized. Even as the light faded around his feet, 41 was moving—weapon drawn—to put his back to the garden wall and to survey his surroundings quickly. Beaulieu stood in the

9

road with a dismayed grimace on her dark face and pulled her
clothing away from her skin.

"They told us it would be hot here, but no one said anything
about muggy. Ugh!"

Ignoring the doctor, Kelly crossed the road to join 41. "Put
the gun away," he said patiently. "This is a very civilized
Alliance world that doesn't allow ordinary citizens to carry
weapons. You've got to keep yours out of sight."

41 frowned, but he obeyed. "Old habits," he muttered.

Kelly said nothing more. 41 had been jumpy ever since they
rescued him off Methanus. Beaulieu said he needed time to get
over what he'd been through, but Kelly knew that on a mission
nervousness tended to become catching.

He activated his comm. "Phila, everyone's down okay."

"Is it a long walk?" she asked, her voice sounding tinny
through the effects of the scrambler.

Kelly glanced at Beaulieu, who had taken bearings on her
scanner and looked even more disgusted than before. "Yes,"
he said. "Crossing town is going to take a while. No evidence
of any surveillance, however."

"Watch yourselves," said Phila. "We've got the waver
shield engaged, and Siggerson is taking us out to maximum
orbit height. Check in every half hour."

"Kelly out." He shook down his cuff over the wristband and
smiled at his two companions. They looked different in their
civilian clothes, softer-edged somehow, and unfamiliar out of
uniform.

Beaulieu, of course, could give flair to even a lab smock.
She wore a vibrant shade of purple silk cut into narrow trousers
and a flowing, wide-sleeved tunic over them. The color
enhanced her black skin, and over her short, no-nonsense hair
she wore a spangled net that shimmered in the newest style of
holo-weave.

41, tall, still too thin although he had fully recovered from
surgery, had tied back his shaggy mane of blond hair and wore
conservative but well-cut neutrals in a shade of dark green. The
practice of using clothing to indicate what kind of job a person
held, where a person lived, and the income a person made had
gone out of style recently. Opulent distinctions were out;

neutrals were in. Only the quality of tailoring gave any clues.

Kelly himself also wore neutrals, even better cut, and in navy blue. The three of them looked like sophisticated city dwellers of the medium executive level. They had credentials to support their appearance if they were stopped and questioned for any reason.

Banqot was a small seaport town on the Minzanese colony world Tunake. Its population consisted of mostly shopkeepers and those who catered to seasonal tourist trade from inland cities. Flying scavengers flapped and fluttered overhead, crying out harshly. There was the pungent, damp smell of the sea mingled with the air pollution of the town itself, not unpleasant exactly, but very different from the sterile, rather stale, recycled air of spaceships and stations.

They had chosen a good time of day to arrive. Banqot's streets were full of pedestrians that spilled off the walkways onto the traffic lanes, and it was easy to blend in with the rest of the population. Horns blared shrilly at traffic jams. Public transportation looked a bit shabby and inadequate. Many people rode simple bi-wheels that ran on magnetic pulse.

Pausing on a corner, Kelly and 41 pretended to look at a hologram of the shop's wares while Beaulieu took a discreet reading from her scanner.

"We need to turn north, then angle toward the east side of the bay," she said.

Kelly nodded. "Any surveillance snoops showing up?"

She slipped the scanner into a pocket. "None that are registering."

"Good."

They left the bustling business district and walked through a distinctly seedy area that would soon need condemning, then passed through streets where renewal and restoration were going on. The houses thinned out again near the far tip of the bay. Here, the streets weren't as well maintained. The traffic got quieter and less hectic. There were more bi-wheels, mostly ridden by elderly people. The sea crashed noisily on the other side of the sea wall. Children yelled and ran about a small park. Periodically a buoy horn sounded from out in the harbor. A large derrick platform with a spidery looking bridge ruined the view of the sea.

They paused near the park to take final bearings on their target.

"The blue house at the end of the street," said Beaulieu, palming the scanner. "And surveillance is crisscrossing us like crazy."

"Stop scanning," said Kelly. His gaze made a slow, seemingly casual sweep of the area but spotted no one watching them. Monitors mounted on floaters would be too obvious out here. Stationary cams?

A Minzanese woman walked past them. She held the hands of two small children, one on either side, and was very pregnant. She did not acknowledge Kelly and his operatives, but her gaze slid cautiously their way.

"Pity," said 41 when she was out of earshot. "This is a peaceful place. I do not want to destroy it."

Kelly sighed. "We don't have any choice, do we? Might as well get it over with."

"Security is poor," said 41. "We have been spotted. We are in plain sight. No one has responded. They are sloppy."

Kelly had to agree with that bleak assessment. If this was any example of how Melaethia was guarded, then she was wide open for snatching or assassination. So much for fervent promises of protection from Minzanese officials.

Kelly started down the street. 41 and Beaulieu followed in silence. 41 kept glancing back, obviously expecting trouble. None came their way.

Kelly frowned. This was too easy.

The place looked small and unimpressive from a distance. Close up, it had thicker walls than usual. The low garden wall running about the boundary of the property had subsonic alarm frequencies set on maximum sensitivity. 41 opened one blade of his prong and performed a quick, incisive jab to one of the receptor nodules. The whole system shorted out.

"Cheap," he said with scorn.

The electronic lock on the gate was just as easy. They approached the entrance of the dwelling, which was built low to the ground with weathered blue walls and a dark roof. The ground was pure sand, much scuffed and littered with wind-carried debris of twigs and cottony seedlings from nearby trees. A few clumps of dune grass stood like tall sentinels.

Kelly stepped onto the porch mat and felt the slightly itchy sensation of a force field activated before him. He pressed his hand against it and felt invisible resistance. No electric shock, however. That was probably a safety measure for the children.

After a few seconds, a synethesized voice came on: "State identity and business."

"Hello, Melaethia," said Kelly. "This is Kelly, Dr. Beaulieu, and 41 come to visit you. We are alone. If your scanner shows more individuals than us, don't open the door."

Seconds became minutes. Kelly frowned and glanced over his shoulder. "Isn't she home?"

"My scanner registers life signs inside," said Beaulieu. "41 probably scared her out of her wits, shorting out the alarm system like that."

41 grunted. "A useless thing should be destroyed. It was wasting energy."

Kelly heard a click and swung around to face the door. A quiet, feminine voice said, "Kel-lee?"

"Yes, it's Kelly," he said. "Sorry to come unannounced like this, but it's important."

The force field deactivated, and Kelly's hair stopped feeling like it was standing on end. He stepped forward, and the door slid open. Beyond it, half-concealed in the shadowy interior, stood a slender figure. Kelly saw the glint of a hand gun and drew in his breath sharply.

"We're armed," he said. "Is your scanner registering that?"

"Step inside, one at a time," she replied. "Make no sudden moves. I have a Watcher."

Kelly's eyes met 41's with amused approval. So Melaethia was better guarded then they had supposed. Watchers were state-of-the-art private protection devices fitted either to individuals or to home security systems. AI programming and sophisticated bioware allowed Watchers to think almost independently. They were programmed to recognize certain persons by heat patterns, retinal scans, and encephalograms. If a Watcher did not recognize someone, it attacked, usually with laser-enhanced precision. Because it could fire from any security nodule linkup within the house, escaping a Watcher was almost impossible.

"I must manually override its activation programming," said Melaethia. "Enter slowly, one at a time."

"Understood," said Kelly. He went inside as though walking on eggs, unconsciously holding his breath, and hoping Melaethia knew how to work the system.

Nothing blew his head off, however, and he drew in a fresh breath with relief once he stepped past her. Beaulieu came in after him, her eyes wide and serious. 41 hesitated a moment, then followed.

Once he was over the threshold, the door slid shut behind him, and green lights came on in a rapid pattern across the complicated control board of the security system. The force field was back in place.

"Now," said Melaethia, turning off a small vid screen, "you are all entered into the Watcher's programming memory."

She turned to face them with a shy but warm smile. "Welcome, guests. I have great surprise and pleasure at this visit."

She had learned to speak Minzanese fluently, Kelly knew from having read the update on her file. Now she was speaking Glish to them, but with a heavy Salukan accent and a tendency to use the formal, stilted Minzanese speech patterns. Despite the dim light within the entryway, he could see physical differences in her as well.

No longer did she wear her head shaven in the style of Salukan aristocrats. Her hair was jaw-length, a reddish-brown shade, and braided into hundreds of thin plaits that bounced and swung attractively with every movement of her head. Her narrow, sharply angled face could never be considered lovely in Kelly's eyes, but by Salukan standards, she was beautiful. In the two years since Kelly had seen her, she had grown radiant and matured into even more grace and poise. Even dressed in a simple houserobe of pale blue cloth, she exuded femininity. In the small space it was almost overwhelming.

She put away the weapon inside a small, inlaid chest and held out her hand in the Minzanese way of greeting.

Kelly took her fingers, and felt the slight prick of vestigial claws. By contrast her skin was warm and as smooth as silk. She wore a subtle perfume that made him blink in an effort to keep his head clear. Apparently her training as a royal concubine was not something that wore off easily.

She smiled as though to him alone, then greeted Beaulieu in the same fashion. 41, however, stood aloof, and Melaethia merely inclined to him without making a closer approach.

"Come into my receiving room," she said. Her soft voice held pleasure that was beginning to overcome her surprise. She led them through a narrow doorway into a room that was small but comfortably furnished in the Salukan fashion. Wooden chairs fitted with thick cushions, brass lamps wrought in intricate shapes, a bare wooden floor, shutters on the windows that let in the sea air yet maintained privacy. A pedestal in the corner held the mother-stones of the household. Even the mingled scents within the room recalled memories of Gamael, home planet of the Salukan Empire. Kelly sniffed cooking spices from the rear of the house.

"Sit here and here. I shall bring refreshments."

Kelly frowned. "Melaethia, this isn't a—"

"Please sit." With a smile, she went through another doorway, leaving them to look uncomfortably at each other.

41 paced the room slowly. Beaulieu raised her brows at Kelly.

"I hate this," she said. "She seems happy here. Why do we have to ruin it?"

"She is lonely," said 41, joining them only to wander away again as though he could not bear to be still even for a moment. "And we have not much time. Let us do it and go."

Kelly glanced at his own chron. Beaulieu turned to watch 41 pace by.

"Why do you say that, 41?" she asked. "How do you know she is lonely?"

41 glared at her briefly. "Pheromones."

"Oh," said Beaulieu.

Melaethia reappeared with a large serving tray of drinks. "I have a pot of hot copra and orange juice. Please sit and enjoy. Which would you like?"

Kelly looked into her face, aware of the shining pride in her eyes, and hesitated. "Melaethia, we—"

"Please," she said, and now there was a hint of strain in her voice. "I am doing the proper custom for Earthers, yes?"

"Yes, you are," said Beaulieu and sat down. "Of course we'd love to have something to drink. I am very thirsty after that hot walk."

"Yes, the heat is of a difficulty," said Melaethia, putting down the tray and passing a plate of tiny, thumb-sized pastries that looked as though they were smothered in honey. "Very different than Byiul. I did not know there were different kinds of heat. When I was asked where to live, I said only a hot place with water. I thought it would be like Byiul, but it is not."

Kelly and Beaulieu exchanged glances. Homesick, thought Kelly. Whether she would admit it or not, she was very homesick. That could be a problem.

"I'll have orange juice," said Beaulieu, and accepted a glass. After a taste, she said in surprise, "It's fresh!"

Melaethia beamed, clapping her hands gracefully at the look on their faces. "I have pleased you. When I came here, I learned of how much Earthers like this fruit. It cannot be exported from Earth fresh, yes? But it can be grown on colonies such as this one. The Minzanese are less strict than the Earthers on agrarian controls."

Beaulieu drained half her glass. "It's delicious. I haven't had any in years."

Kelly also accepted some. It was chilled and he was thirsty, but he visited Earth more often than Beaulieu did. Minzanese varieties of the fruit varied not only in size but in flavor from the original. This had only a ghost of the taste of what his mother would have served at her breakfast table, but he smiled and complimented Melaethia, who beamed even more happily.

"41?" he said. "Better have something."

"The cakes are wonderful," said Beaulieu, licking her fingers. "Are they a Salukan recipe?"

Melaethia inclined her head slowly. "Yes, but I am afraid I do not cook well."

"You've done an excellent job with these. Kelly, try them," said Beaulieu, passing the plate again.

41 came over but did not sit down. Kelly noticed that
Melaethia grew quieter in his proximity and kept her eyes
downcast in a modest, careful manner when she spoke to him.

"*Ai vau copra ivi, achei,*" he said in Saluk.

In silence Melaethia poured the spicy drink for him and held
it out in a way that guaranteed their fingers made no contact as
he took the cup from her. 41 shook his hand in refusal of the
pastries and wandered back to the windows again, sipping the
stuff as though he was used to pouring pure fire down his throat
every day.

Kelly caught Beaulieu's eye. She raised her brows meaning-
fully.

"Melaethia," he said slowly. "We practically broke into this
place. Where are your guards?"

The light faded from her eyes. Her shoulders stiffened
defensively. "I have none."

"Why not?"

"It is a great expense. Great trouble. When I came here, they
watched for a time. But this town is small. Everyone knows
everyone. It is hard enough to be a Salukan here without
causing questions to be, but it is ever harder with guards. I
have to live normal in my ways. I cannot be a prisoner
forever."

She clutched her glass and frowned, her eyes full of an
emotion Kelly could not read. "If you have come to make
again me a prisoner, I—"

"Melaethia, I didn't mean to criticize," he said quickly. "It
was just curiosity . . . and concern."

Some of her defensiveness eased away. "Then you did not
come to check on me? You came for pleasure of being guests?
This is a great honor. Salukans enjoy hospitality very much. I
have not often had honor of giving pleasure to guests."

Kelly frowned. This was getting harder. He didn't want to
hurt her feelings, but it looked like he couldn't avoid it.

"I'm sorry we haven't come before, Melaethia," he said. "I
don't think many of us understand Salukan customs. It is our
way to leave people alone unless they request otherwise."

"You have strange ways," she said. "I watch many vids and
slowly I learn, but there is the Earther way and the Minzanese

way. They are not the same, and it has been the Minzanese way I was to be learned first." She frowned slightly. "When my father lived, things were different. We spent much time with the Earthers. Now . . . I like the quietness of Banqot. I am given peace here. My neighbors do not concern for me."

An odd silence fell over them. Kelly finished his juice, aware that he had to get down to the real reason they were here.

"How are your children?" asked Beaulieu, still using the sociable, pleasant tone that she'd adopted since walking into the house. Kelly wondered if all women were programmed at some point in their lives to utilize the social rituals of making small talk, complimenting refreshments, and admiring off-spring.

Melaethia smiled and once again looked shy. "They are well. This time is when they sleep, but if you are very quiet you may see them."

Beaulieu glanced at Kelly. He gave her a slight nod and she stood up. "Yes, please."

Melaethia rose as though floating to her feet. She smiled at Kelly. "Is it also your wish to see my son and daughters?"

"I would be honored," he said, "but I—"

"Kelly," said 41 from the window. "An aircar just landed."

Kelly jerked to his feet. "Identify the occupants."

41 shook his head. "Not in sight yet."

"Melaethia," said Kelly, "are you expecting any visitors?" She looked frightened. "No," she said, almost inaudibly.

Kelly eased past the furniture to the windows and peered through the thin gap between shutter slats. Beyond the low wall, the aircar sat parked. No one got out.

"Scanning us," said Beaulieu.

"No!" said Melaethia in disbelief. "I have a jammer—"

"Doesn't work, honey," said Beaulieu. "We took several readings on you ourselves."

Melaethia's cheeks darkened to bronze. She opened her mouth, then shut it without a word. Abruptly she ran to the rear of the house.

"Do I follow?" said Beaulieu.

Kelly nodded. From the corner of his eye he saw that 41 had

drawn his weapon. "Don't start shooting yet," said Kelly.
"Beaulieu, give me the scanner."

She tossed it to him and disappeared in the direction
Melaethia had gone. Kelly switched on the hand-scanner and
watched the readout for several seconds.

"Four of them in the aircar," he said. "Minzanese readings."

41 grunted but did not put away his gun.

"They're opening a comm line," said Kelly. He switched off
the scanner and entered the foyer to activate the vid. By then
all he got was a brief squawk signifying end of transmission.

"Damn! I missed it."

41 eased from the window and glanced about the room as
though judging its defense capabilities. "They are coming
now."

Kelly looked out and saw four burly Minzanese exiting the
aircar. They held discreet-sized Humoc heat-seeking repeaters
that could be hidden within their clothing.

"Alliance-issue weapons," said Kelly. "I'd better talk to
them—"

"Wait," said 41. "Not yet—"

Melaethia returned with Beaulieu at her heels. Melaethia
threw Kelly a reproachful glance. "Not enemies," she said.
"Colonel Sushif Non. Please do not cause trouble in my home.
I must turn off the Watcher and let them inside."

Kelly's gaze went to Beaulieu, and she said, "There's a vid
in the back room and a sophisticated security scanner. They
passed Melaethia's system checks. They're on our side."

"You are too much worried about my safety," said Melaethia. "The Salukans do not care about me now. Such guarding
is not to be a necessity."

She opened the door and let two of the Minzanese enter. The
other two remained outside by the aircraft, alert and scanning
the area.

"Welcome, Colonel Sushif," said Melaethia. "Come into
my home."

Sushif was nearly as broad as he was tall, his upper body
looking absurdly top-heavy for his short legs. His drab olive
uniform was pressed into razor-sharp creases. He carried no

obvious weapon. The Humoc in his grim assistant's hands made one superfluous. He did not wear the usual hair tassels favored by most of the tradition-loving Minzanese race. His short-cropped hair was straight and black, with a slightly green cast to it. His eyes were the same as cops' eyes anywhere, of any race, in any corner of the galaxy.

They went to Kelly and stayed there, boring in. "Identification," he said in Glish.

Kelly produced his AIA IDent card and handed it over. Sushif hardly glanced at it before passing it to his assistant, who examined it closely.

"Commander Kelly of Allied intelligence," he said, making it a declaration. "I am Colonel Sushif Non, Banqot Law Enforcement."

"Delighted, Colonel—" began Kelly, but Sushif waved amenities aside with an impatient gesture.

"All visits of Allied Intelligence Agency must be registered with Banqot law enforcement," he said. "All weapons checked in."

As he spoke he was glaring at 41, who made no move, either to surrender his gun or to put it away.

"This is a Code 30 assessment," said Kelly. "We have clearance to be in Tunake orbital space from Tunake Defense Central—"

"Planetwide jurisdiction does not concern Banqot jurisdiction," said the colonel stiffly. "Banqot not informed. This not procedure acceptable. You are in violation of civil law."

"And what about yourself, Colonel?" retorted Kelly, deciding he'd had enough of this stiff-necked squat. "We entered city perimeters, passed full surveillance snoops, penetrated this security net, and entered this house without any response from your department."

Sushif's face grew even stiffer. "Am here now."

"Yeah, twenty minutes later. We could have killed her and ransacked this place and been gone within five. You're sloppy. Melaethia says no one is actively guarding her. The Minzanese government promised—"

"What is promised on Minza is not always done on Tunake," said the colonel.

"Obviously."

Melaethia stepped between them. "Please," she said in distress. "You are both misunderstanding—"

"Unless you have acceptable authorization for presence here, you will leave in custody," said Sushif.

"They are guests, Colonel Sushif," said Melaethia. "They helped my father and me to defect. My life is owed to them."

The colonel glanced at her briefly and bowed, but his attitude did not unbend. His eyes went right on boring into Kelly.

"I've told you we have a Code 30 assessment—"

"I have no proof of that. All I see are unauthorized Intelligence agents in Banqot, where such personnel not permitted without stringent controls. All carrying arms. That is against Banqot law. You have—"

"Here," said Kelly, producing a scrap of flimsy from his pocket. "This is what I showed Tunake Central. Will it satisfy you?"

The colonel read the brief orders with a frown. He handed it back to Kelly. "I must have this checked."

"Go right ahead," said Kelly. "41, put up the gun."

"You will surrender your weapons," said the colonel.

"Not likely," said Kelly in a very mild voice.

The colonel glared at him for several seconds. Kelly met the look and didn't back down. Finally the colonel blinked and snapped an order to his assistant, who left the house and went hurrying back out to the aircar.

Kelly looked at Melaethia, who showed a mixture of alarm and growing anger. He gave her half a smile. "I'm sorry," he said. "We didn't intend matters to get this mixed up. Everything will be clear soon."

"I do not know about clear and mixed up," said Melaethia curtly. "I see rudeness. I see my home filled with guests who do not honor it. I see Minzanese interference with how I live. I will have my guests sit, Colonel. I do not consider you a guest today."

He bowed in silence, his expression not changing. Kelly preferred to go on standing, but Melaethia gestured imperiously at the chairs. Kelly and Beaulieu sat down with her. 41

remained in his corner by the window, his gaze flat and hostile.

Kelly looked at Melaethia, aware that he'd better explain everything to her before that assistant came back and blurted it all out. "Melaethia," he said quietly, but urgently. "I need to tell you the real reason we're here."

She gestured angrily. "No explanations. I will offer you more juice."

"Melaethia—"

She glanced away. Kelly saw Sushif watching them suspiciously and felt his own temper beginning to fray. "Melaethia, I must—"

The assistant returned breathlessly and murmured for several moments in Sushif's ear.

"Hah," said Sushif when he finished. "Very well, Commander. Tunake Central says you have clearance to leave before dusk. This woman and her family also have clearance. I am not to interfere. Make certain you are prompt. We do not welcome visitors, unofficial or otherwise, who do not observe protocol courtesies."

With a final bow to Melaethia, the colonel and his men left.

Even as the door slid shut, Melaethia was rising to her feet. Her face was dark bronze with anger; her eyes flashed at Kelly.

"What does he mean, leave? I do not leave my home! This is my place. My father earned it with what he did for the Alliance. You cannot take me from here."

Kelly also stood up. "Melaethia, this isn't permanent. The Alliance Council wants to talk to you and they—"

"And am I closed in my comm receiver to them?" she retorted haughtily. "Can they not ask me in a manner courteous? Why must you come, pretending to be guests, pretending to be friends, when you are really Earther arrogance to order me here and order me there."

"Melaethia—"

"You even take food from me. Insulter! I will not have this treatment—"

"*Aret chese!*" snapped 41, loud enough to silence her. Before she could gather another angry breath to continue, however, he crossed the room and seized her by the wrist.

She slapped at him, but he caught her other wrist and held

her in place. Yellow eyes glaring into her dark ones, he spoke
to her fast and furiously in harsh Saluk, most of it too fast for
Kelly to understand. Then he released her with a little shove
and stalked from the room.

"41," said Kelly, but he was gone as though he had not
heard.

Kelly swung back to face Melaethia, who was standing with
her arms wrapped about her abdomen, her eyes dark with
anger, her face stricken.

"No one has the right to speak to me in that way," she said
in a low voice of fury. "Not even those who save my life. My
mother was of a major house. I have borne three children to the
Pharaon, three children who carry the true, royal line. And
that—that abomination whose existence is an affront to the
very gods dares to call me a fool. He dares to remind me that
I owe blood-debt to the Alliance and to you, Kelly. He makes
me a child again, to be ordered this way and that, lacking my
own will, subject to what I am told."

She tossed her head, making her plaited hair bounce. "Tell
me this, Kelly. Would you have said the same words to me?
How long did you intend to accept my hospitality before you
let the lash fall? I might as well be an Earther slave as live here,
pretending to have freedom."

"Melaethia, I don't know what exactly he said to you," said
Kelly, trying to hard to keep his own temper when he wanted
to go after 41 and cut him down to size. "We came to see you
because we've been ordered—"

"*Suh!*" she said.

"Let me finish! Raumses is dead."

Her eyes went wide, and all the color drained from her face,
leaving it a sickly shade of yellow. "The usurper is dead?"

"Yes. That's still classified information, by the way. Not
even Sushif knows about it. Most of the Alliance is still
uninformed and will be for some time. The Salukans have not
yet made it officially public within the Empire."

"His heirs?"

Kelly shook his head. "No heirs."

She sank down in a heap, missing the nearest chair and

hitting the floor with a thud. Beaulieu reached for her, but Melaethia lifted a hand and Beaulieu backed away.

"It was a military coup," said Kelly. "Raumses was murdered, as far as we can tell. There's a lot of confusion, and our information is sketchy in places, but we think it's an attempt to reestablish the order that existed before Nefir's death."

"Before I killed him," said Melaethia hollowly. She spread out her fingers. "They will come hunting for me. They will avenge his murder. While Raumses lived, I had safety. Now . . ."

"Not necessarily." Kelly rammed his fingers through his hair. "I was supposed to wait and let members of the Council discuss this with you. But it may be that the Salukans will want you back."

"To execute me!"

"Or to honor you as mother of the new Pharaon."

She looked up at Kelly in shock.

He said gently. "Your son is the only living heir of Nefir. It's a possibility that we must prepare for."

"You would make me go back?"

Kelly heard the naked fear in her voice and knelt beside her. He gripped her arms although he was aware it was probably a Salukan taboo to do so. "No one will make you go back," he said firmly, meeting her eyes. "No one."

She seemed to drink in reassurance from him, then her eyes grew wild again. "Not my son! You will not let them take him from me!"

"No one will take him from you," said Kelly. "You have the word of the Alliance on that."

She spat.

"Melaethia." He waited until she met his gaze again. "You have my personal word as well."

Slowly she pulled away from his grasp and rubbed her skin where he had touched her. "You kept your word before," she said. "My father trusted you and you did not fail him. You risked your life for us."

"It's only for your own safety, Melaethia," he said. "The Council wants you to understand all the political ramifications of what is happening. They want you to be fully informed.

They want you protected from any attempts at assassination . . . or kidnapping."

She nodded. "This I understand. It is just that it is my home. Mine. Before, I lived at the choosing of others. I had to please others to keep my place. Here I say what is and is not. Here I need not wear a veil and conceal myself."

"I'm sorry," said Kelly gently. "Sometimes we just can't be left alone to live as we choose."

She did not meet his eyes. "I shall go with you, Kelly."

"Good." He pulled a teleport wristband from his pocket and handed it to her. "Put this on. Dr. Beaulieu has some for the children. We haven't much time. Doctor, help her get them ready."

"Come," said Beaulieu. "They should be awake during teleport. Otherwise it might scare them too much. We've tried to prepare a nursery on board our ship, but they'll need some of their own things. Please show me what you want to take."

Melaethia got up. She frowned. "You ship is so small for all of us."

"No, we have a larger ship now. Come," said Beaulieu and went with her into the back of the house.

41 reappeared from the galley, and Kelly whirled on him.

"What the hell did you think you were doing?" he said before 41 could speak. "Who told you to jump in and tell her like that? You damn near got her mad enough to refuse to listen to anything I said."

"She was not listening before I spoke," said 41.

That was true but Kelly was too mad to admit it. "Your job is to do what you're told and to shoot when it's necessary. You aren't a diplomat, and you—"

"Kelly, she was manipulating you. She is manipulating you still," said 41 harshly. "It is her way. She was trained to do it. Why do you think the Pharaon's concubines are shut up away from everyone but the Pharaon himself? Because they have strong effects on men. She was making you pity her. And now she has you defending her. She needs neither."

Kelly blinked, not certain whether to believe this or not. "She never affected us that way before."

"She was pregnant. Now she is fertile again. And dangerous." 41 snorted. "I do not want to talk to her, and I will not do it again. But I warn you, if you will heed it, that the Alliance Council had better talk to her with women."

"I'll pass that recommendation along," said Kelly dryly. "Why don't you call the ship and tell them we're almost ready to come up?"

From the rear of the house came a loud wail from one of the babies.

41 scowled. "I shall do it from outside."

"Don't you like babies, 41?"

41 paused at the door to glance back. "No," he said, and left.

2

Dominate a child too soon and it will be weak. Dominate a child too late and it will bring shame upon its father. Spare not the swift reprimand and let there be laughter in the home.

—from the Scroll of Tees

Salukan babies were ugly.

Melaethia came herding the three toddlers before her, naked except for their knickers. To Kelly they looked identical from the tops of their narrow, shaven skulls to their bare bony feet. As a rule, Kelly rather liked small children. His experience was that they were plump, sweet-smelling, and delightfully innocent. These, however, were so thin they looked all joints and bone. He could see the cartilage ridges beneath their skin that protected their throats and lower abdomens. They were hissing in ill temper, and three sets of beady, hostile eyes glared at Kelly.

He took an involuntary step back as they passed him to enter the receiving room. One of them lunged at him, but Melaethia caught the child by the arm.

"Do not bite!" she said sharply in Saluk. "Sit!"

Another one darted across the room. Melaethia went after it. She grabbed it about the middle and lifted it, kicking and hissing and shrieking, to carry it back and settle it in a chair with its siblings. Beaulieu appeared, carrying a large duffel bag. One of her sleeves was ripped, and she had an angry

27

scratch on her cheek. She met Kelly's gaze without a word and
dropped the duffel bag beside Melaethia.

"Better we had let them finish their nap," said Melaethia
breathlessly as she struggled to fit a screaming, squirming
toddler into a pair of small coveralls. One of them bit her on the
arm and she cuffed it. "*Aret!*" she said angrily, and it hushed
in mid-cry.

When she had them dressed, she glanced over her shoulder
with her hair in her eyes. "The wristbands?"

Beaulieu handed them over. "Put them on their legs," she
suggested.

"No, here is better," said Melaethia and fastened the bands
around each small throat. Shoving her hair from her face, she
glared at Kelly. "And you have the proper food on your ship?
Routines are important. I will not let them be upset in the
stomach."

Kelly, who had been thinking they had better rig some kind
of force field around the nursery area, blinked at her.
"Uh . . . Doctor? We're set up for Salukan diet, aren't we?"

"Yes, but it's adult," said Beaulieu.

"*Suh*," said Melaethia and headed for the galley. "I must get
some—"

"Make her hurry," said Kelly to Beaulieu.

The doctor glared at him. "She's upset and it's communi-
cating to them. Why don't you take the babies on up to the
ship? They'll all probably feel better if they're separated for a
few minutes."

Kelly had the dubious feeling that it would only make things
worse. But Beaulieu stalked off into the galley. He could hear
her talking to Melaethia. There came the sound of something
slammed in reply.

Sighing, Kelly eyed the toddlers who by now were out of the
big chair and scattering in three directions. He activated his
comm. "41?" he said. "Get inside. I need some help."

The minute 41 reentered the house and saw Kelly struggling
to hang onto a kicking, screaming child that was doing its best
to bite him, he threw back his head and laughed.

"Dammit, 41!" said Kelly in exasperation, juggling the brat
and terrified he was going to drop it, "do something!"

41 reached down and scooped up the child that was trying to dart past him to get outdoors. At once the child hissed in fury and started clawing, but 41 flipped it tummy down and set his teeth gently upon the back of the child's neck. It quieted, and so did the hellion in Kelly's arms.

A little startled by 41's solution, Kelly nevertheless drew a breath of relief. Holding one, he crossed the room and plucked down the third triplet that was teetering on the back rim of a chair.

"How long are you going to bite its neck like that?" he finally asked.

41 grunted and raised his head cautiously. "His neck," he said. "I have the son."

"Do you? I can't tell them apart." Kelly juggled until he had the little girls settled, one on each hip. He looked critically into their homely little faces. Two sets of dark eyes stared back. This close, he saw that one had deep purple eyes; her sister's were truly black. "Are you sure they're girls?"

"Can't you smell the difference?"

"Oh," said Kelly blankly. "I guess not."

41 stared a long moment into the boy's implacable eyes until he dropped his gaze, then 41 tucked him under one arm like a sack. "When do we go?"

"Beaulieu thinks we ought to take the kids up without Melaethia. She says Melaethia is upsetting them."

41 came over to stand beside him. The triplets exchanged glances.

"Uh, 41?" said Kelly, feeling the dig of tiny claws as the purple-eyed girl clung more tightly to his arm. "Do I need to assert dominance over these the way you did him?"

"No," said 41. "Once is enough."

Since Kelly had both hands full, 41 called the ship. "Bring us up, Phila."

The teleport beam caught them, and when they materialized on the *Sabre*, all three children started to cry.

Phila Mohatsa, the youngest member of Kelly's squad and the electronics specialist, jumped to her feet in startlement. "*Mandale*! What the hell—uh, begging your pardon, Commander—is all this?"

"Babies, Phila," said Kelly in exasperation, coming off the platform with both girls screaming in his arms. He juggled them up and down, trying to distract them, but their little faces were turning dark and wrinkled, and they weren't about to be comforted. "So much for Beaulieu's ideas on child handling. Here, take one."

He stuck one at Phila, who drew back involuntarily. Tiny but a bundle of energy, normally Phila didn't shrink from anything. She reached reluctantly for the child, which hissed at her. Phila jerked her hand back.

"Forget it," said Kelly, changing his mind. "You'd better get Beaulieu and Melaethia up here as fast as possible. Give them a call and tell them, ready or not, they're coming up now."

Phila dropped back in her chair without bothering to disguise her relief. "Yes, sir."

While she got busy, Kelly glared at 41. "How do we shut them up?"

"They are frightened," said 41. "They are too far to sense their mother. It is good for them to know separation for the first time. But they will not stop crying until she comes."

"Phila," said Kelly in desperation. His ears were starting to ring with the noise. "Bring them up."

"Teleporting now."

Blue and silver light flashed upon the platform, and Melaethia and Beaulieu materialized. Melaethia came running off the platform almost before she was entirely there. She stumbled as a result and would have fallen, had 41 not caught her with his free arm. Their eyes met briefly, and he snarled something hateful in Saluk before shoving her away.

She took her son from his arms, her face pale, and comforted him. As soon as he began to quiet, the girls did too. Both of them reached out their thin arms to their mother. Aware that she couldn't possibly hold all three, Kelly clung to them.

"We might as well get you settled in now," he said. "Phila, inform Siggerson that we're ready to leave orbit. And be sure he notifies Tunake Defense Central first. We've stepped on enough toes for one day."

"Uh, right," said Phila.

"Welcome aboard the *Sabre*, Melaethia," said Kelly with a smile for their guest, who did not smile in return. "Come this way, please."

She followed behind him, not at his side, although he paused more than once to allow her to catch up. Her eyes remained angry, and her face was set in a way that told him she did not mean to relent. He wondered if they had made matters worse by taking the children up without her. Probably.

Kelly sighed. He couldn't wait until this mission was over.

41 came after them, carrying Melaethia's two duffels. He kept a far distance, however, and did not even approach the door of Melaethia's guest quarters until she had entered. Then he tossed the duffels just inside the door and vanished.

Kelly put down the little girls, steadying them on their feet. They darted away from him before he could unfasten the teleport bands. One glanced over her shoulder and hissed defiance at him. He smiled, but without much amusement.

"When you remove the bands, Melaethia, they should be returned to the teleport bay."

Melaethia glanced around. She had a bunk and three cribs, which had caused a lot of consternation in Station 4's quartermaster office in trying to find some that met combat ship specifications. There was also a head and a tiny sitting area which had been supplied with toys that Kelly now realized weren't sturdy enough.

Bending, Melaethia picked up a soft-bodied doll and stared at it as though she had no idea of what it was.

Kelly hesitated, tempted to explain, then decided to avoid the whole issue. He pointed at the wall. "Here's the in-ship comm. Just call if there's anything you need. You're on the second deck now. All the living quarters are here, along with the sickbay and the mess. Someone will call you when it's time to eat. You can, of course, visit the mess at any time you wish, but we generally prefer to eat together for social reasons. You have the run of the ship. I would prefer, however, that the children be confined to this deck. The bridge is on deck one, and the engines are on deck three. They don't need to be in either location for their own safety."

She stared at him in silence.

He frowned. "Do you have any questions?"

For a moment he thought she would still refuse to speak, then she said, "Can the half-one be kept off this deck?"

"His name is 41," said Kelly sharply.

"He is of a great rudeness. I do not wish him here."

"I apologize for his manners," said Kelly although it was difficult to keep annoyance from his voice. "But all the living quarters are on this deck, as I've just explained. He has just as much right to be in this area as he does anywhere else on the ship."

Her chin came up imperiously. "I do not wish him near my children. He tried to dominate my son. He had no right."

"Perhaps not. But at the time it seemed necessary." Kelly glanced at the children, who were busy exploring the place, fingers into everything. "They're pretty lively, you must admit."

"It is a great offense. This must not occur again."

"I'm sure he didn't understand that he was being—"

"He is a savage. Make him understand."

Kelly's temper nearly escaped him, but he held it down. "Very well," he said mildly. "I'll inform him. But I doubt that you need to worry about his interaction with the—"

"I will *not* worry," she said. "It will *not* happen again."

Kelly saw no point in continuing to placate her. "Anything else?"

"No. Not now."

"Then I'll leave you to get settled. Sometimes time distort is upsetting to children. They shouldn't eat until we've jumped. Make sure they're well strapped down. I'll have you notified before we—"

"Thank you," she said. "We shall be alone now."

Annoyed by her dismissal, but relieved to finally get away, Kelly strode out. He didn't care for being ordered around on his own ship, and Melaethia would have to remember that whatever fancy privileges she'd enjoyed as a royal concubine no longer applied. Maybe finding out she was the mother of a potential Pharaon had gone to her head. He hoped she reverted to a better mood soon, or he was seriously tempted to confine her and her brood to quarters for the duration of the voyage.

In the privacy of the corridor, he touched the scratches on his neck and arm. Some had broken the skin. He frowned and headed for sickbay.

Beaulieu was at her post, already changed back into her uniform. "Is Melaethia any calmer?"

"Icy." He sighed. "I hate diplomatic missions. Do you have any disinfectant?"

Beaulieu smiled. "Scratches or bite marks?"

He pulled up his sleeve. "A few nicks."

"Worse than mine." She opened a storage locker and pulled out a sealed canister of swabs. "I've never been the maternal type, although sometimes I've regretted not having children. But not today." She swabbed his arm gently, and some of the sting faded at once. "How about you, Kelly? Determined now to stay a bachelor for the rest of your days?"

He chuckled. "We may all be child haters before we get to Earth. I've always liked kids. Now I'm going to amend that to human kids. If these are typical Salukans, no wonder they grow up to be so fierce."

"Pretty typical, I'd say. Melaethia told me they weren't trained yet. This whole business has really upset her."

"Can't blame her. By she's in a wicked mood. I had trouble keeping my temper. Thanks, that's better." Kelly pulled down his sleeve. "By the way, 41 says she's dangerous to the male population right now."

Beaulieu's brows went up. "Dangerous?"

"His choice of words, not mine. Here're some more: fertile and lonely."

"Oh, God. And that automatically makes her out to snare any male in sight, I suppose." Beaulieu snorted. "Sometimes I think 41's mind is positively medieval."

"He may be right."

"Kelly!"

"No, listen to me," said Kelly. "I tangled with a Salukan female when we were on Gamael. She used telepathy or some kind of mind control. I'm not saying Melaethia will try that, but she isn't human. There's a lot we don't know about Salukans."

Beaulieu still looked skeptical. "Human or Salukan, men are

pretty much alike. Why don't you turn Caesar loose with her? He's the Casanova of the space lanes, or so he claims."

Kelly laughed. "Test 41's theory, you mean? I don't think so. Beaulieu, I'm not trying to be chauvinistic. I'm just mentioning it, because if any of us start acting peculiarly I want you to be on the alert."

"You're serious about this, aren't you?"

"Yes, I am. I like Melaethia. But that other female I mentioned nearly killed me before I got away from her. I'd rather we be cautious than sorry."

"All right," she said with a shrug. "I'll keep it in mind if you start howling at odd hours. Actually, if you're really worried about Salukan ways, you might keep your eye on 41."

"What do you mean?"

"Since when has he drunk copra or spoken Saluk willingly?"

Kelly blinked, startled by her suspicions. "I thought he was being sociable."

She laughed. "41?"

"You should have seen him at my brother's wedding. He can act civilized when he chooses to."

"That I find hard to believe. But you know how much he hates the Salukan half of his heritage. For him to be acting even vaguely Salukan is odd."

Kelly frowned. "You think Melaethia is attracting him?"

"Who knows? I'm just reporting my observations."

"Well, she ordered me to keep him off deck two."

Beaulieu laughed. "You're kidding. That touchy?"

"At her very worst."

Beaulieu's amusement faded, and she grew thoughtful. "Well, Kelly, you might consider it."

"Come on!"

"I'm serious. Salukans have fairly violent mating rituals, don't they?"

He shuddered involuntarily. "Yes, but these two don't act attracted. From what I've seen, they hate each other."

"In humans that's a dead giveaway. In Salukans?" She shrugged. "They've each given warning, in their own way. Whether it's love or war, who knows?"

"All right. I'll talk to 41," said Kelly slowly. "But it may just make things worse. He's already avoiding her as much as he can."

"Maybe," she said.

"Don't be cryptic, Doctor."

She shot him a quizzical look. "You asked for advice. That's all I have."

"Well . . . thanks," said Kelly. He started for the door, then reached for the comm instead. "Kelly to bridge."

"Siggerson here," came the reply. "We just cleared Tunake space. Do you want us to jump now or wait until we're out of the solar system?"

"The quicker the better, Mr. Siggerson," said Kelly. "I want us on the most direct route to Earth, best possible speed."

There was a slight pause as though Siggerson was doing some calculations. "Very good," he said at last. "I have astrogation computers running that now. We'll be up to jump velocity in twelve point two minutes."

"Good," said Kelly. "Notify all hands. Kelly out."

As he broke the connection he glanced over his shoulder at Beaulieu. "I've warned Melaethia of what to expect during jump. She may need some help."

Beaulieu scowled. "I may be a doctor, but that doesn't make me an expert babysitter."

Kelly opened his mouth, but before he could say anything, she added, "Oh, all right. I guess I can administer a light sedative. But if another one bites me, I'll—"

"You'll spray some skin mesh on and do your job," said Kelly firmly. He looked her in the eye. "Won't you, Doctor?"

She snorted, and he went out with a grin.

A short time later, Kelly emerged from the lift onto the bridge, feeling better now that he was back in uniform. He found the bridge humming quietly with activity. Olaf Siggerson sat at the master station, his lanky shoulders hunched over the controls, his eyes calmly monitoring the mix of manual and automated as the ship responded to his expert touch. Ouoji lounged along the top of his control boards, apparently asleep, her silky gray fur ruffling slightly in the air circulation. Phila had 41 sitting at her station, patiently explaining to him how to man the long-distance scanners.

Siggerson glanced up, nodded at Kelly, and said, "One minute to jump. Phila, announce it."

"Hokay." She reached over 41's shoulder and made a curt announcement, then noticed Kelly. "Commander, what's with the formality?"

Kelly activated the main viewscreen. No matter how many times he went into time distort, it was always a treat to watch the blur of the light spectrum.

"In case you've forgotten, we have guests aboard. Small guests, who aren't used to traveling TD."

"Oh." Phila shook back her curly black hair which fell unbound to her shoulders. "I forgot about them. Do babies get space sick?"

Kelly was spared answering by the barely perceptible shudder in the *Sabre* as she shifted from impulse to photonic drive. They soared over the curve of space into a breathtaking rainbow of color. The stars blurred and shifted, and the universe turned shades of blue and violet as the aberration effect spread the light spectrum.

Then Siggerson adjusted the viewscreen to a simulacrum, and the constellations became normal again. Kelly blinked, making the momentary adjustment from that dazzlement of the senses. Phila gave a small sigh of satisfaction, and he smiled at her, aware that she loved to watch jump even more than he did.

"Achieving TD 1," said Siggerson's laconic voice from behind Kelly.

"Good," said Kelly. "Push her on up."

"Accelerating. We'll have TD 12 in about forty-eight minutes. No point in upsetting the passengers."

"Nice and smooth," said Kelly. "That'll do."

"Hey, Siggie!" called a loud voice from across the bridge. Caesar came in, laden down with a belt of tools, grease smearing his face. His red thatch of hair was rumpled as though he'd had his head stuck into a tight space. "I found that vibration. Can you tell a difference?"

Siggerson's bony hands flew over his systems checks. "Not registering now. Where was it?"

"One of the feeds between the reserve batteries and the light scoop. I told you it wasn't much."

"I want to have a look at it myself," said Siggerson with a frown. "I told you just to locate it, not fix it."

Caesar came up and leaned his elbow upon the master station. "Well, I did fix it, Siggie-boy, so relax. I'm not totally thumbs."

"That remains to be seen. Switching to full automateds now." Siggerson hesitated and glanced at Kelly. "Do you want us running with the waver shields on?"

"41," said Kelly, "anyone showing up on the scanners?"

"One freighter, robot-class, about four hundred thousand kilometers," said 41.

Kelly approved. Since he had expressed an interest in learning to operate the ship's sensors, 41 had shown himself a quick pupil. "That's in the space lane?"

"Shipping lane 12-Alpha for this sector," said Siggerson. "We can dispense with the waver shield. No point in squandering energy if we don't have to."

"Better stick to procedure," said Kelly. "I'd hate to be caught with our pants down."

"Right." Siggerson engaged the waver shield and stood up. "I want to look at this repair job."

Caesar rolled his eyes in mock exasperation. "What's the matter, Siggie? Think you're the only one who can do anything around here? When are we going to jump, by the way? Or are we running on impulse all the way to Earth?"

"Idiot," snapped Siggerson. "We've been in distort for almost—"

"Wait a minute," said Kelly, breaking in. "Caesar, didn't you hear the announcement?"

Caesar shrugged his stocky shoulders. "Nope."

"That's ridiculous," said Siggerson sharply. "The comm's almost directly over the—"

"Didn't hear it," said Caesar. "So what? Since when do we bother? Did I miss a drill or something?"

Kelly frowned at Siggerson. "That comm unit shouldn't be malfunctioning. Is there isolated circuit failure?"

"I'll check." Siggerson scratched his balding head and went back to his station.

"Hey," said Caesar, looking a little uneasy. "It's no big deal. It's just a—"

"Definitely circuit failure," said Siggerson icily. He turned on Caesar, who held up his hands and backed away. "What did you do?"

"Okay! I shorted out a couple of things in there. The probe slipped. It wasn't any—"

"You fool!" said Siggerson furiously. "It's bad enough that you were adjusting a line feed during a jump, but if you had shorted out something crucial, we could be spinning into infinity at this very moment with no hope of ever getting back. Are your brains so pickled with alcohol consumption that you've lost all sense? You—"

"Siggerson," said Kelly.

"Sir, he really should be—"

"That will do, Siggerson," said Kelly. "Go check the damage."

Siggerson glared and strode off the bridge. It had gotten very quiet. Phila was making certain she looked busy. 41 was watching openly. Kelly turned his gaze upon Caesar, who went bright red in the face.

"Now, boss, I'm not drunk. And I didn't mean to—"

"Siggerson is right," said Kelly quietly enough, but with an edge to his voice. "You endangered all of us. And you know better than to be that careless. Caesar, what the—"

"I'm sorry," said Caesar hoarsely. "It's just that Siggerson goes around like he's the only one on board who knows anything about engineering, when Phila's just as good as he is at putting stuff together. And it was a simple repair. I know not to touch equipment I'm not qualified to maintain. I could handle it, and I did."

"Why didn't you report the short out as soon as it occurred?" asked Kelly. "You knew we were preparing to go into distort."

"Well, no, sir. I—uh—I mean we were in orbit when I crawled back there. I thought I had plenty of time to—get it fixed. Siggerson was supposed to be on standby for your signal, so I knew he didn't need to be in the battery room.

Usually the ship lurches when it goes into distort. But Siggie was so smooth today, I couldn't tell."

He was lying. Kelly had known Caesar long enough to read all the signs. "Weren't you watching the feed line you supposedly were repairing?" he asked. "Didn't you notice the increase in utility consumption?"

"Uh . . . I guess not."

Kelly's eyes narrowed. "Your story has enough holes to fly through, Mr. Samms. I want a—"

"Commander."

It was Siggerson, standing in the doorway with his fists on his hips, looking even more disgusted than before.

"Yes, Mr. Siggerson?"

Siggerson held out his hand. Caesar's breath sounded strangled. Without looking his way, Kelly headed toward Siggerson.

"A bleed coupler," said Siggerson furiously.

Kelly picked up the part. It was about the length of his palm, two fingers wide in diameter.

"It was lying inside a slot hole in one of the bulkheads," said Siggerson. "You've been stealing energy, Samms. What for?"

Caesar turned red again. His eyes went wide in appeal to Kelly, then flashed defiance. "You ain't the commander around here, Siggerson. I don't answer to you."

"Kelly," began Siggerson hotly, but Kelly held up his hand.

"Thank you, Mr. Siggerson," he said in an absolutely neutral voice to cover his deep anger. He put the coupler in his pocket and looked at Caesar, who frowned miserably. "I'll expect a full explanation in my quarters in ten minutes, Mr. Samms."

"Yes, sir." Caesar hurried into the lift and vanished.

"Why?" demanded Siggerson. "You've given him plenty of time to finish hiding or destroying any evidence, not to mention think up a story. We had him here red-handed with this—"

"That'll do, Siggerson," said Kelly.

"Playing favorites is a poor way to run a—"

Phila shot to her feet. "Shut up, Siggerson! You're going too far."

Siggerson's mouth closed in a thin, set line.

"Thank you, Mohatsa," said Kelly, still in that quiet, even voice. He glanced at her, and the look in his eyes made her pale. "I believe I can handle this alone."

"Yes, sir," she muttered and sat down.

Kelly returned his attention to Siggerson. "We'll finish this discussion in my quarters, twenty minutes from now."

"You'll—"

"Please be prompt," said Kelly.

Siggerson started to protest, then apparently thought better of it. He met Kelly's eyes briefly and looked down. "Yes," he said reluctantly. "I'll be there. But I—"

"Phila," said Kelly, "you are in charge until I return. 41, you stay on duty as well."

Fuming, Kelly stepped into the lift. They were supposed to be the best squad in the Hawks, and a few weeks ago when they banded together to rescue 41 from the cyborgs on Methanus they had been an efficient team. But since they all came back from leave, they'd been pulling in independent directions as though they'd never heard of teamwork.

Although delivering Melaethia to safety was crucial, this mission lacked enough challenge to put an edge back on them. Dammit, if they stayed this sloppy they could end up guarding ore freighters for the rest of their careers.

He didn't intend to let that happen.

3

When Than, mischief maker of the gods, throws his knuckle-bones among the stars, even the constellations topple. It is a time for luck, either good or bad.

—School Manual, general mythology

Kelly went through his spacious quarters quickly, cleaning his discarded clothes off his bunk and tossing them into the recycle chute. Scarcely had he seated himself at his desk than the chime sounded at the door.

Kelly's hands closed into fists which he rested on top of his desk. He sat with shoulders military straight, his back like a ramrod.

"Come in," he said, and his voice was harsh.

Caesar entered slowly, lacking his usual bounce. He had changed into a clean uniform, shaved, and wiped the grease off his face. His unruly red hair had been slicked down severely. As he walked up, his gaze went to the coupler lying on Kelly's desk. Kelly saw him swallow.

"Okay, boss," he said glumly. "We don't have to go through the whole routine. You know what I was using it for. And I know you know."

Five years earlier, on a different ship, with a different squad, Kelly had caught Caesar distilling liquor and bootlegging it. The still ran off ship's power, and the power bleed was so small

41

that Caesar had gotten away with it for several months before he was caught.

Now Kelly looked at him in disappointment, wondering what had prompted him to do such a stupid thing again. "Why?" said Kelly. "A dare? A bet? Boredom? What in God's name made you pull a midshipman stunt like that? You don't have to bootleg liquor. You have access to just about anything, and I don't restrict off-duty consumption the way some commanders do."

Caesar's expression grew stubborn. "No excuse, sir."

"I want an explanation. Caesar, you can bleed power off old-style implosion engines, but with photonic drive you risk killing us all. I might overlook it if I understood, but unless you tell me the truth I'll have to report you for this one."

Caesar tucked in his chin and said nothing.

"And," continued Kelly grimly, "strip you of rank and privilege and confine you to quarters for attempted manslaughter."

"Hell!" said Caesar in startlement. "It's not that bad."

Kelly stared up at him implacably. Caesar got away with a lot from him. They'd served together too many years for it to be otherwise. But this wasn't just a prank. It was a dangerous piece of carelessness or indifference that could not be ignored.

"You really would," said Caesar slowly. "After all we've been through, you'd really lop me off, just like that? I never thought I'd live to see the day when you'd turn on an old friend."

Kelly slammed his fist on his desk. "Dammit, Caesar! What do you expect from me, when you nearly killed us? If the *Sabre* had blown up during jump a few minutes ago, would you have said oops?"

Caesar's face went red. "I didn't risk anyone's life! Yusus, if you believe that you've really gone off the pike."

Kelly frowned. "You'd better remember who you're addressing, mister."

"Don't give me that discipline of the service crap, Bryan," said Caesar. "I worked the still while we were docked in Station 4. Just once, for old time's sake with my pals. Thom—uh, someone wanted a demonstration of how it's done. I know better than to pull a power bleed on an operating photonic drive. All I did was tap the reserve batteries a little. But it was my fault that we had that little vibration. I didn't reset the tap-in plates in precise alignment, see, and so I volunteered to do the repairs before old sour-puss Siggerson found out what I'd been doing and ran to rat on me." Caesar scowled. "Just like he did anyway. But no one was at risk today. You can put me through a truth verifier scan if you want."

"I see." Kelly's frown deepened. He didn't need the scan. "And why didn't you say so immediately, instead of letting me think—"

"Well, why did you immediately believe the worst of me? Treating me like I'm some bone-headed squat who can't find his ass with both hands," said Caesar hotly. "Why did you believe old Siggerson, braying his suspicions like a—"

"Enough," snapped Kelly.

Anger burned in his face, but he knew better than to start justifying himself. As soon as he could control his voice, Kelly said quietly, "You won't go on report. Since I didn't find you working a still while we were on the inactive list at Station 4, I can't put you under severe discipline. However, since you were stupid enough to leave incriminating evidence lying around for Siggerson to find—"

"He had to look bloody hard to find that coupler," said Caesar angrily.

"—and the whole squad knows about this, I can't look the other way. You're getting full demerits."

"Boss!"

"It means a dock in pay for a full quarter."

"But, boss—"

"Shut up," said Kelly. "You broke regulations and you got caught."

"And what about Siggerson?"

"What about him?" asked Kelly icily.

"You going to pat him on the back and throw a party in his honor for ratting on me?"

Kelly didn't like the bitterness in Caesar's voice, or what it implied. He rose to his feet. "Mr. Samms, you seem to have forgotten that you are in a military organization, with rules, an oath that you were sworn to uphold, and penalties for failure to remain within the boundaries of your duties and responsibilities. I suggest you spend the rest of this duty shift cleaning the engines and re-inventorying our arsenal while you do some serious thinking about the fact that you're in the Hawks to serve, not to be a duffel-headed clown."

Caesar opened his mouth, then closed it very tight.

"That's all," said Kelly.

In silence, Caesar wheeled smartly on his heel and strode out. Siggerson was waiting at the door to come in. He did so slowly, his eyes watching the stiff set of Caesar's shoulders. Kelly looked for a sign of smug satisfaction and found it in the brief quirk of Siggerson's lips.

Anger snuffed out the last of Kelly's self-restraint. "Siggerson," he said coldly, "you seem to have a grudge against Samms. Would you care to explain that?"

Siggerson looked startled. Looked guilty. Reluctantly he approached Kelly's desk. "I have no explanation," he said stiffly. "You're mistaken."

"I know when something's going on between my operatives," said Kelly. "And there's a problem between you and Caesar that wasn't in existence before we went on extended leave. I want to know what that problem is. And I want to know now. We can't operate as a team unless we're all pulling together. A squad in opposition is a squad that gets killed."

"Really," said Siggerson, "I don't think we're in any danger at this moment—"

A violent lurch threw Siggerson off his feet. Only Kelly's quick grab of his desk kept him from falling as well. The ship lurched the other way, rocking as though she'd collided with something. That time, Kelly went tumbling.

Overhead, the alarms sounded. Through the blaring noise, the comm squawked: "Kelly and pilot to bridge! Kelly and pilot to bridge! We have a—"

The comm went dead. Kelly scrambled to his knees, wondering about circuit failure, wondering what the hell was happening. But before he could get completely to his feet, the lights went out.

The darkness seemed to suck him into it, pitch black and

absolute. The almost subliminal hum that was the life of the
Sabre ceased, and fear caught Kelly in the throat one split
second before heat, air, and gravity failed as well.

For all intents and purposes, the *Sabre* was dead.

No gravity was the immediate problem, although it was far
from being the most serious.

Floating toward the ceiling, Kelly struggled to keep himself
oriented in the darkness. "Siggerson!" he called. "You all
right?"

No answer.

"Siggerson!" said Kelly sharply. "Siggerson, wake up."

Still no response. Kelly bumped into the ceiling and spread
out his arms, groping gently for emergency rungs to hold onto.
He felt the urgent need to find out what was wrong with
Siggerson, what had happened to the ship, and pinpoint the rest
of his people, but he forced himself to make no sudden
movements that might send him spinning out into the center of
the room.

His fingers touched a rung and curled over it. Clinging there,
he struggled to figure out his position in relation to the door.
With the power out, the door should be open, but in the
darkness he couldn't verify that.

He finally decided it must be in the direction his feet were
pointing.

The emergency rungs criss-crossed the ceiling in two
straight lines. Floating on his back, with his face bobbing
against the ceiling, Kelly shifted himself from rung to rung,
holding his feet pointed downward at a thirty degree angle to
miss the soffit over the doorway.

He was beginning to pant a little by the time one of his feet
hit a solid obstruction and the other one didn't. The door was
partially open. Kelly wiped the sweat from his face and thought
a moment.

With eleven air breathers on board, roughly double the usual
ship's complement, they had about two hours of oxygen within
the ship itself, providing everyone remained quiescent and
there were no hull leaks. One hour beyond that in environmental suits. After that, there were only the stasis beds in the

emergency life pods, and they might float suspended for all eternity before they were found.

The temperature was already falling. He shivered lightly and swung himself through the doorway.

In the corridor, he turned himself so that he faced the wall to the left of the door and traced with his fingertips until he found the emergency locker set into the wall. Normally its sensor plate would have responded to the brush of his fingertips, and it would have popped open. He had to dig his fingers into the shallow recess and pull on the small door to get it open.

Slipping his hand through the contents net that kept things from floating out in a null-gravity situation, he rummaged inside blindly, seizing the square hand torch. Thumbing the button brought a sharp beam of light that lit up the corridor. Kelly's spirits rose automatically. He was just reaching for a communicator when the light faded and went out, plunging him back into pitch blackness.

Kelly frowned, stunned by the failure. He shook the torch without avail. It was supposed to have a heavy-duty charge pack inside it, with a life expectancy of about fifty solar years. Still frowning, he tried the communicator.

"Kelly to . . ."

The faint hum of the communicator faded out. He thumbed it hard, several times, but couldn't raise even a squawk of static on it.

"Damn!"

He chucked the equipment back into the locker and shut it. In the distance he heard a faint sound. Kelly froze, straining his hearing.

"Caesar?" he called. "41?"

"Kel-lee!" said the frightened voice of Melaethia from down the corridor. A child whimpered, only to be quickly shushed.

"Melaethia, don't panic," said Kelly, making his voice firm and assured. He propelled himself down the corridor toward her, keeping one hand on the wall for guidance. "Stay in your quarters."

"What has happened?" she said. "I cannot see you. We—"

"Any of the children hurt?"

"No, I—I do not think so."

"Good." Kelly snagged a rung and stopped his impetus a short distance away from her. His only guide was the sound of her voice. "Stay inside your quarters and strap them down in safety harnesses."

"But they want to—"

"No," he said firmly. "Gravity could come back on at any minute. That's when there will be injuries." He thought briefly of Siggerson, apparently floating unconscious in his quarters, whom he had not secured before he left. "Do as I say, Melaethia. I have to see about my ship. I can't stay with you here."

"I do not ask for that," she said scornfully. "I want to go with you."

"Stay here," he said. "I don't need an amateur in the way."

She made no response to that. He was sorry to resort to rudeness, but he couldn't afford the time to argue with her. Again, he propelled himself along the corridor, but this time he misjudged his velocity as well as the distance and slammed into the emergency ladder.

For a moment the pain was sharp, catching him in a frozen breath of agony. He thought his collarbone was broken, but cautious movements showed him it was not. Relieved, he finally sucked in a full breath.

Was the air already tasting stale? He shoved away the illusion of not being able to breathe and pushed off, aiming vertically up the ladder well to deck one.

"Who is it?" called a tense voice from the bridge.

Phila's voice. Kelly created a mental image of her in his mind: small, wiry, intense. Her black eyes would be wide in her face. Her curly hair would be floating in a dark nimbus around her head.

"It's Kelly," he said, and could feel her relief roll over him in a wave.

"Sir, what—"

"Give me a report," he broke in sharply. "Did we collide with something? What caused the power outage?"

"I'm not sure," she began doubtfully, then her voice sharpened and grew quicker as though she could sense Kelly's impatience. "We were still on the acceleration curve Siggerson had plotted. 41 picked up something on the distance scanners. He couldn't identify it. We had nothing on the viewscreen. I got a glimpse of what he was reading just before we hit. Something like an energy wave. I—I don't know how to explain it. We seemed to hit a wall of energy. Then we lost power."

Kelly frowned. He didn't recognize the technology she was describing. "Where's 41 now?"

"He went down to the engine room. I've been trying to get us switched to auxiliary battery reserves, but so far even the emergency torches won't work."

"I know. The communicators won't either," said Kelly. "It's like we're under a power damping field. We'd better try to find a—"

Something warm and furry brushed his face. Kelly slapped reflexively to knock it away and succeeded in sending himself drifting backwards. He bumped into the wall and by then felt embarrassed.

"Sorry, Ouoji. I didn't realize that was you."

Ouoji chittered at him through the darkness. He felt her paw tap his cheek, then her tail curled around his throat like an anchor. She chittered again, anxiously.

He touched her silky fur. "I know. We'll get this problem figured out somehow although what 41 thinks he can do in the engine—"

Ouoji tapped his face again, chittering urgently. He got a sudden, vague sense of danger.

"Phila," he said quickly, "are we losing hull pressure?"

"I can't check, sir," she said, but he'd already realized that and was annoyed at himself for the lapse.

"I'd better get down there. Something is—"

A tremendous cry rose from the depths of the ship, echoing up the ladder well on a surge of terror that made the hairs on Kelly's neck stand up.

"That was Caesar," he said, staring wide-eyed into the darkness. He had never heard a sound like that come from Caesar before. Reflexively, Kelly drew a prong from his leg pocket. He snapped all three blades of the stiletto open.

"Come with me," said Kelly over his shoulder. "We'd better stay together."

"Yes, sir."

He started down the ladder well without waiting for her to find her way across the bridge. The silence of the ship had taken on a menacing quality. He found himself listening to his heartbeat going slightly too fast, listening to the jerk and exhalation of his own lung rhythm. His hand felt sweaty on the prong handle.

Ouoji still kept her tail around his throat, letting his impetus pull her along with him. He heard Phila blunder into the ladder well and he wanted to shout at her to be silent. But he didn't waste the effort. He strained to hear what was ahead of him.

A heavy thump—felt through the metal core of the well rather than heard—made Kelly pause. A long shudder ran through the ship. At once he knew the difference. It wasn't the *Sabre* coming back to life. She was being acted on. Something had docklinked with them.

"Pirates," he said to Phila.

"Wha—"

"Come on!" he said furiously.

He kicked hard to propel himself faster, and only his outstretched hand kept him from slamming himself into the deck at the bottom of the well. He rolled, curling his arms and legs in the way learned long, long ago in Academy null-gravity simulations.

There was light, a backwash of it that shimmered golden and soft into the well from around the corner. Kelly pressed himself against the wall, and with his free hand caught Phila as she came plunging down.

He pressed his palm over her mouth before she could speak. Her face was a dingy blur in the gloom of the well. He looked into her eyes and held up his prong. She nodded and drew hers from her sleeve.

Down the corridor came a sound that again made Kelly's skin prickle inside his sleeves. A slurred chink of sound. The sound of magnetic plates sliding over, then locking down upon the deck. Space suit sounds.

Kelly's breath stopped in his throat. He pulled Ouoji off his

shoulder and left her floating. Easing himself forward, he left
the well like a shadow, trying to keep himself flat against the
wall, although his body wanted to float into a horizontal
position.

He could feel the tight drum of anger pounding in his
bloodstream and his mind raced furiously. What pirate group
had the technology to catch up with a photonic-drive ship,
much less stop her in her tracks? Who would be insane enough
to cross space untethered between the two ships and board
through an access hatch? How the hell had the boarders
breached the hatch without losing internal pressure and atmosphere? How many were there? How many were they about to
let through the main airlock? What kind of damping field were
they using that didn't affect their own equipment? *Who were
they*?

Pressing himself against the wall, he peered around the
corner, fraction by fraction, until he could see them. Three
figures, bulky in environmental suits of shabby black with
scratched power tanks strapped to their backs. One was busy
applying an illegal lock-breaker to the airlock's security
circuitry. One was holding Caesar pinned against the wall, a
device held at his throat that did not look like a weapon yet
must have caused that scream. The third was standing as an
observer, its back to Kelly, almost close enough to grab.

At the other end of the corridor, Kelly glimpsed a shadow
move into the backwash of light, then retreat. But the observer
spotted it.

Before he could do more than step forward, however, Kelly
launched himself. He caught the observer high in the back,
driving his prong between the shoulder blades with a stabbing
slash that let out the suit's atmosphere in a cold whoosh of
stinking air. With a howl of anger, the observer twisted, trying
to pin Kelly to the wall, but Kelly kicked himself up toward the
ceiling and swarmed over the observer's head, attacking hose
feeds, helmet and visor plate in a fury.

The other two came at him, but Kelly managed to rip off the
observer's helmet before they seized him by his legs and arms
and pulled him down. One stamped upon his right wrist and his
prong fell from suddenly numb fingers. Kelly barely registered

it. He was too busy staring up into slitted eyes of malevolent orange, a furrowed brow plate, two holes where a nose should be, mashed, concave cheekbones lacking anything resembling a zygomatic arch, and a slack, brutish mouth full of too many crooked teeth to fit within it.

Despair mingled with fury came welling up in Kelly. They'd been taken by Jostic raiders, taken as easily as a defenseless passenger liner, and unless it was in the mind of these brutes to sell them, not a single person on board the *Sabre* had a prayer of survival.

4

The forge of the battlefield . . . the hammer beat of attack. For this we live. For this our blood sings hot.

—warrior's song

The Jostic observer seemed to enjoy the effect he had on Kelly. His lips stretched, showing even more teeth—some of which were rotted stumps—and he gave Kelly a kick. The other two Jostics pulled Kelly upright. Floating between them, he struggled, trying to wrench free, but they slammed him against the wall and held up one of those small, box-shaped devices that they'd been using on Caesar, who was now a crumpled heap floating near the floor.

Before the device touched Kelly's throat, however, the thin, pop-crack sound of a Gert percussion pistol went off. The observer screamed in agony. His companions whirled around, and Kelly saw the observer clawing at his face. Blood gouted freely in a thick, spiraling stream that drifted into the air. Another shot struck him in the throat, striking sparks off the metal collar of his space suit.

The observer, still clutching his bleeding face, sank halfway to his knees. His boot plates had him anchored to the floor and only null-gravity supported him. With a moan, he let one of his hands drift down limply.

One of the others bent over him with an inquiring grunt.

52

Kelly took advantage of the distraction. Curling up his feet and using his back against the wall for leverage, Kelly kicked the Jostic's faceplate with both heels as hard as he could. The Jostic swayed back, but his boot plates kept him from falling. Rolling forward, Kelly kicked off from the wall and tackled him, slashing at helmet and air feeds.

The Jostic twisted beneath Kelly's assault and pressed the device to Kelly's shoulder. Agony flashed through his nerve endings and straight out the top of his skull. For a moment Kelly thought his head had exploded. He heard himself screaming, and there was nothing he could do against the pain which froze him helplessly.

Then the pain switched off, as abruptly as it had come. Gasping, Kelly glimpsed 41 and the second Jostic grappling savagely. 41 was using his prong with quick, in-and-out slashes that cut the environmental suit's circuitry but didn't get past its armor.

Kelly rolled himself over to go and help, but his opponent caught him by the ankle and pulled him back. Kelly put up no resistance, using his backward impetus to crash into his opponent. Kelly grabbed his helmet. With a wrench he succeeded in twisting it off. The Jostic hit him in the chin, dislodging him and knocking him back before he could use his knife.

Kelly rolled to avoid the floating globe of blood and slammed into the wall. He tried to grab a rung before he ricocheted the other way, but missed it. Frustration didn't help. Kelly forced himself to concentrate, and the next time he bumped into a wall, he made sure he got hold.

He found himself near Caesar, who was dazedly pulling himself together.

"Caesar," said Kelly breathlessly, "you okay?"

"Yo," said Caesar although his eyes weren't tracking well. He was so pale his freckles stood out starkly, and there was an ugly burn mark on his throat. "Ganging up on . . ."

Caesar's voice failed on him in a coughing fit. But Kelly saw the two Jostics getting the better of 41. There was a lot of blood polluting the air now, but most of it was the wrong color.

"Need one little blast," said Caesar darkly. "One . . . little . . . bomb."

Normally Kelly wouldn't countenance one of Caesar's bombs going off onboard the *Sabre*. But now, with the two Jostics about to subdue 41 and active sounds of cutting coming from the other side of the airlock, he shot Caesar a hopeful look.

"What have you got?"

Caesar grinned and tried to reach inside his tunic, only to have his arm spasm violently. Still keeping one hand on the rung, Kelly grabbed him with his other.

"Easy, easy," he said.

Caesar's teeth gritted, and the cords in his neck stood out in his effort to stop the spasm.

"Don't fight it, Caesar," said Kelly. "Try to relax."

"P-pocket," said Caesar. The shakes started to ease off, and he closed his eyes.

From across the corridor, 41 cried out in pain. Goaded, Kelly thrust his hand into Caesar's tunic and pulled out a small round ball of a hard, shiny substance. It wasn't moldable, like most explosives. It wasn't the gel stuff that Caesar favored.

Kelly figured he could find out the particulars later. "How do I activate it? And how close can I throw it without killing 41?"

Sparks flew from the control panel of the airlock, startling all of them. One of the Jostics abandoned his hold on 41, now floating motionless, and shuffled toward the airlock. As he passed Kelly and Caesar, they hugged the wall, watching him warily. His orange eyes slid their way and gleamed, but he went straight to the airlock and reactivated the code breaker.

Because the locking circuits were already frying, the code breaker shorted out as well in a spectacular show of green, gold, and blue sparks that sent the Jostic staggering back, waving his arms and spluttering.

If things hadn't been so serious, it would have been funny.

A series of muffled thumps on the other side indicated that the rest of the raiders were coming through.

"Boss," said Caesar softly from one side of his mouth, "it's heat activated. Keep squeezing it in your hand, but make sure you have your finger pressing that small indentation or it'll go off."

Hastily Kelly rolled the ball over until he found the indentation. Sometimes Caesar was just too damned casual with this stuff.

"When they come through, I'm going to throw it," Kelly whispered grimly. "Get ready to fall back. Head for the arsenal. How fitted are we with percussions?"

"Not much," said Caesar.

With a terrible grating noise, the airlock slowly cycled open. A bulky figure in a black environmental suit poked in its head. Kelly held his breath, waiting, waiting, making sure he had the right moment to get as many of them as possible. He thought about asking Caesar how severe a blast this bomb would produce and whether it would blow out the airlock and kill all of them, but he didn't.

An advanced ship like the *Sabre* couldn't fall into enemy hands, especially Jostic hands. Kelly knew his duty, even if he had to destroy his own ship, and he meant to carry it out at any price.

He let the first figure enter. Others appeared, stepping through slowly, gazing around through black-tinted faceplates. One finally grunted and gestured at those behind him.

They were still clustering together, but at any moment they were going to string out along the corridor. Kelly lifted his hand, gauging the moment.

"Now, boss," whispered Caesar at his back.

Yes, the lead Jostic was turning, taking the first step. Kelly threw the little bomb in an easy lob, right into their midst.

Caesar's fingers dug into Kelly's shoulder. Kelly gave a strong kick to launch them away.

Two things happened: the bomb exploded, and the power and gravity came back on.

Lights and weight, a great, deafening roar and gush of scorching heat. Flying, yet falling, hitting the deck hard and tumbling over and over. Smells of burned metal and flesh. A shrill ringing sound punctuated by screams of pain.

Urgency drove Kelly up through the dazed mists of shock concussion. He was on his hand and knees before he was fully conscious. He tottered over, and hitting the deck this time woke him up. His ears still rang.

He felt a hand tugging at him. Kelly squinted and saw Caesar through the smoke. With a grunt Kelly climbed upright and staggered forward.

He couldn't seem to track in a straight line. The end of the corridor kept moving closer then farther away. Caesar's lips moved. The sound of what he was saying came in slow motion, slower than the movement of Caesar's mouth, and was garbled through the ringing in Kelly's ears.

"So mon, surrey up. Surrey up! Feed you get out."

"Food?" said Kelly, frowning.

He nearly stumbled over 41's leg, then realized Caesar was bending over 41 and trying to shake him awake. The blood that had been floating in the air previously now lay splashed upon the decks and walls where it had fallen. Jostic blood. It stank.

41 sat up, nodded to Caesar, and got to his feet. He and Kelly exchanged glances, and with a frown 41 grabbed Kelly's arm in a tight grip. He said something, and his words were just as garbled as Caesar's.

"Don't worry," said Kelly, trying to reassure him. "You'll be better directly."

"Hoodoo dearie?" said 41. "Dearie?"

"No, I'm not your dearie," said Kelly.

41 grabbed him by the chin and looked closely into his eyes. Some of the confusion cleared from Kelly's mind.

"Hoodoo hear me?" said 41. "Do you hear me?"

The ringing faded somewhat and 41's words caught up with his mouth. In relief, Kelly nodded. His improved hearing, however, brought him sounds of groans and stirring near the airlock. Kelly turned, half-unwillingly, to see the destruction he'd wrought and glimpsed a figure moving within the airlock.

There was a shout of anger, and a plasma bolt missed Kelly's head by centimeters. 41 yanked Kelly to one side, and they were running, zigzagging crazily up the corridor, their backs exposed. Ahead, Caesar scooped up the small Gert pistol 41 had used earlier. It was strictly short range, with soft bullets that could not pierce bulkheads or inner hulls. Kelly wasn't certain it could pierce body armor either, but Caesar started

shooting back to cover Kelly and 41, and that slowed down the
second wave of pirates for a few seconds, long enough at least
for them to round the corner and gain the dubious shelter of the
ladder well.

Caesar tossed the Gert to 41 and went up the ladder like a
madman, pausing several rungs up to open a circuit panel and
flip breakers. "That shuts off the lifts," he said, panting. "Now
they can't beat us to the top."

Kelly realized his brain was still rattling around too loosely
inside his skull. He needed to sharpen up, and fast. "Good
thinking. Let's—"

41's hand gripped his sleeve. Kelly turned and saw 41
peering down the corridor. The stiff alarm in his body made
Kelly tense up too. He flattened himself to the wall and eased
his head around the corner just enough to see.

Five more Jostics were coming cautiously through the
airlock, stepping over the mess that had been their companions. And in the midst of them stood a Salukan in civilian
clothes, shielded only by a force belt. He held a blaster in his
hand.

Now Kelly understood exactly what was going on. This was
no random pirate raid. These Jostics were in Salukan employ,
come to take Melaethia and the triplets. They had Salukan
technology, and they had used a very sophisticated damping
field to capture the *Sabre*.

Kelly swallowed. It was no longer simply important that
they keep the *Sabre* from being taken. It was vital.

He tapped 41 on the shoulder and motioned at the ladder. 41
waggled the Gert and nodded. He would remain at the base of
the ladder and hold them off for as long as possible. Kelly
frowned. With the limited ammunition of a Gert, that wouldn't
be long.

Caesar was already going up the ladder. Kelly said, "Fall
back to deck two. We'll have to hold them there."

41 nodded, his attention focused on the approaching enemy.
Kelly started after Caesar, moving fast, knowing they hadn't
much time.

The worst of it was that the teleport bay was on deck three,
which the Jostics had possession of. Kelly desperately wanted

wristbands so that he could communicate with his squad and get everyone coordinated. But since that was momentarily out of the question, he would have to chance using in-ship comm lines.

Accordingly, he paused at the second level and used the comm there to call the bridge.

"Phila, listen fast," he said.

"Commander, it's a Salukan—"

"I know. Stand by. We've been boarded. Caesar's on his way to you. Load from the arsenal."

She started to say something else, but he cut her off and called sickbay. No answer.

Frustrated, Kelly hesitated, but the sound of firing going on below him sent him climbing again. He would have to count on Beaulieu being able to hold Melaethia safely in her cabin. Siggerson, whom he'd left unconscious in his own quarters, remained a question mark.

The situation was not good, not good at all, and it was getting worse every minute. Kelly climbed savagely, letting his anger build in order to key himself up for what lay ahead. The *Sabre* was supposed to be the fastest ship in the galaxy. She was technologically advanced. She had superb scanners. She was running with her waver shield on, which meant no one should have been able to detect her. Yet she had been caught like a bug in a web.

It made Kelly feel like a fool. He and his squad had been made to look like a bunch of unprepared bumblers, and they were too good, too well trained for that. It shouldn't be happening, but it was.

Puffing, he reached the bridge, found it deserted, and headed for the corridor beyond, where Caesar and Phila were already at work in the small arsenal.

"Load me up!" called Kelly. "I've got to reinforce 41."

Phila came running to him with two die-hards already assembled and charged, a belt of additional charge packs, two bi-muzzle Maxell pistols that were a bit too powerful for in-ship fighting but could slice through body armor effectively, and some DeFlex grenades.

"Caesar says to only let the grenades charge halfway. That cuts the blast size way down," she said breathlessly.

"We don't want to destroy the ship along with the invaders," said Kelly. "How about force belts?"

Caesar, overhearing, tossed some out into the corridor. Kelly scooped them up and fastened one around his middle. Slinging the die-hards over his shoulder, he looked down into Phila's intense, half-scared face.

"Phila, you get yourself kitted and armed and stay on the bridge."

"But, sir, I want to—"

"It's important," he broke in. "We can't let them have the *Sabre*. The rest of us are going to do our best to repel them, but if they get past us, if they get up here, you must set the destruct."

Phila's face went bone white. She stared at him, her black eyes like coals in her face.

"Go ahead and set up the sequence. Have it armed and ready. You know the drill."

She nodded as though her voice had dried up.

"In the meantime, see if you can do anything through the computers. Maybe set up an override on that other ship's systems and get us free of the tractor net or whatever they're using to hold us. Contact deck two if you can. Use brief communications, scrambled. Try to get Siggerson up here with you. Questions?"

"No, sir," she said. She looked very small, very young.

He squeezed her shoulder and gave her a brief smile. "I'm counting on you, Mohatsa."

Caesar came out, laden with gear.

"You're to hold deck two," said Kelly. "Watch that second ladder in case they discover it. Come on, people. Move it!"

Down the ladder, feet echoing on the rungs, breath coming harder, palms sweating lightly in anticipation of the fight. Firing still going on sporadically below, the sounds distorted from the bottom of the well.

Kelly found 41 still in position, holding on coolly despite a slag burn charring his sleeve.

"That serious?" asked Kelly as 41 moved back to put on a force belt.

41 shook his head. "Missed. Bad shots. The Jostics are getting anxious to attack."

"How many Salukans?" asked Kelly, feeling the familiar hum of the die-hard charging in his hands.

"One. He retreated." 41 bared his teeth as he said it.

Kelly grinned back. "Did you cut a notch in his abdomen plate?"

"Very close." Then 41 sobered. "They have damaged the teleport."

"What? The hell they have."

"To keep us from escaping perhaps?" 41 grunted. "Very stupid Jostics."

"Most of them are," said Kelly grimly. "But they—"

Loud yells made him break off. The raiders were coming. 41 pressed himself to the wall opposite Kelly, his die-hard ready in his hands, his yellow eyes intent with purpose.

But the Jostics didn't attempt to breach the ladder well. Instead they entered the lift, and Kelly heard it engage.

Frustration seared him. "They got it working!"

He broke from cover, firing in a violent sweep as he went. Two Jostics still in the corridor fell, but the rest were on their way up.

Someone returned fire from within the airlock, but Kelly retreated, unwilling to slag that area. He cursed long and hard.

"How many?" he demanded. "Three? Two?"

"Six," said 41. "Six in the lift. More waiting."

Kelly stared at him in astonishment tinged with dismay. "They usually raid in groups of ten or less. You're saying there are at least—"

"This is no ordinary Jostic raid, and we are wasting time," said 41.

Kelly slung his die-hard over his shoulder and started up the ladder. The muscles in his arms and legs were burning with weariness, but he ignored that, driving himself up even faster. Deck two was the vulnerable spot. They would search there first, or would they go straight to the bridge and take it?

He was urgently aware of Phila, waiting up top with her finger on the destruct sequence and her nerves like wires.

The lift stopped on deck two. Kelly heard muffled gunfire, and his heart raced with the need to get there. He launched himself from the ladder well in a diving roll and came up on his feet in the corridor behind the Jostics who were exchanging fire with someone hidden within the battered doorway of sickbay. Kelly slagged them, his plasma bolts melting deep into their suit armor.

Three of the six went down, screaming inside their helmets. The remainder scattered. One was shot by Caesar, who bobbed into sight from sickbay. Kelly fired at the remaining two, but missed. A shot screamed off his force shield, the backlash of energy crackling about him. Kelly threw himself flat, his heart thumping into his ribs, uncomfortably aware that whatever ammo they were using was very close to the maximum his shielding could deflect.

The lift started down, summoned from below. Kelly's heart sank with it. More reinforcements. How many were there?

The two Jostics still in the corridor had taken slim cover behind a bulkhead rib. It was going to be difficult to pick them out, and every passing second gave the enemy advantage.

Kelly signalled to 41 at the entrance to the mess. In the distance he heard a child wail for a moment, then all was quiet again. From his quarters, Siggerson's lanky arm extended and beckoned.

One of the Jostics fired at it, and Caesar lobbed a DeFlex grenade at their hiding place.

Kelly scrambled to his knees, horrified at the risk, but Caesar did indeed manage to get the thing to explode at half capacity. The Jostics went flying, and the bulkhead rib crumpled but did not entirely collapse.

Caesar ran to check on the Jostics, making sure all were dead or too injured to pose future threat. Kelly called, "All clear!"

41 and Siggerson emerged from their positions. Siggerson had a dagger from Kelly's collection in his hand. There was blood smeared on his face, and his eyes held more animation than Kelly had ever seen in them.

"Have those damned brutes reached the bridge yet?" he

demanded before Kelly could start snapping orders. "They'll pick this ship clean. Damned filthy scavengers. They—"

"That'll do," said Kelly, although he shared Siggerson's sentiments fully. "Get up to the bridge, Olaf. Phila will brief you there. Our priority is to break free."

"We'll have to lower emergency bulkheads and seal off the bottom deck," said Siggerson doubtfully. "I'm assuming they blasted through the airlock?"

The lift was coming up. Siggerson ducked into the well and started climbing. Kelly, Caesar, and 41 took stances in the corridor.

"What is this," said Caesar, popping a charge pack and slapping a fresh one into the butt of his die-hard, "last stand at the Watermo?"

"You mean the Alamo," said Kelly, grimly checking his own equipment.

"Nope. Nobody survived that one. Bad luck, boss. Watermoo, that's it. You know the old battle."

"Waterloo," said Kelly, looking at him with mingled amusement and exasperation.

"Soyo," said Caesar with a shrug. "It's Waterloo for the Jostics."

"Not if we don't take the initiative instead of just reacting defensively," said Kelly. He frowned. "We need to cut them off at the knees, get inside their—"

"I'll do it," said 41.

He turned and ran up the corridor in the opposite direction from the lift before Kelly could say anything.

"Hey!" yelled Caesar, glaring over his shoulder. "Come back here, you yellow-haired lux!"

"Can it," said Kelly because the lift was stopping. He braced himself, feeling vulnerable and exposed and mad enough not to care. "Go to work, Caesar."

The doors slid open, and they fired, slagging the surface of the lift and shorting out circuits in a brilliant starburst of sparks. Two Jostics fell, but the others huddled back inside the lift, taking partial cover behind the doors that were now frozen halfway open. They fired back, and Kelly and Caesar dived for cover in opposite directions.

Something numbed Kelly's heel, and he drew his legs under him swiftly as he squirmed himself behind the inadequate protection of a bulkhead rib. Plasma scorched the metal just above his head. He pulled himself lower, wincing from the heat and making sure molten pyrillium didn't drip on him.

Across the corridor, Caesar was firing his die-hard in a series of calm, efficient bursts, keeping the enemy pinned down. They shot back for a few moments, then something ovoid and black came rolling out.

Kelly stared at it in a moment of calm, cold comprehension. "Bomb!" he said.

Caesar shot it a split second before it detonated. Kelly threw himself flat, his arms over his head. The blast shattered the world, seeming to pull the whole guts of the ship down on top of them. Dangerous pieces of metal went flying in all directions. Chunks of wall and deck boiled in the dust and powder. A fire klaxon shrilled, piercing the rumble of destruction and falling debris. Even as he shifted out from beneath the junk that had rained down upon him, Kelly smelled the acrid stench of burning circuits. Then fire burst through the wall, flaming brilliant orange.

Furious, Kelly picked himself up and ran through the blaze straight at the lift, shooting like a madman. Return shots scorched him, missing so closely he felt something sear past his cheek and ear. Not caring, he shouted something incomprehensible and slagged the inside of the lift until nothing stirred at all. Only the click of charge depletion stopped him.

He stood there, breathing the sharp stench of smoke that was rapidly filling the corridor, his eyes hot in his face, adrenaline pounding hard.

A tap on his shoulder. "Boss?"

Kelly swung around furiously, and jammed the depleted die-hard into Caesar's startled gut. "Are you crazy?" he shouted. "Got any other bombs you want to detonate just for kicks? That could have been—"

"It was a crawler," said Caesar quickly, eyes wide with alarm. "Honest to honest, I shot it off early or there'd be a hole in the deck big enough for us to fall through. They're nuts, using a crawler in close quarters like this. Whoever gave them that equipment has scrambles for brains."

Kelly's battle-madness faded abruptly. He felt the sag of adrenaline and let his die-hard dip. Weariness rolled over him and he rubbed his face.

"I must be getting shell-shocked," he muttered.

"Naw, just too many blasts too close together," said Caesar with a grin. "It gets on people's nerves, if they aren't used to it."

Nodding, Kelly moved away and listened a moment, trying to gauge how badly damaged his ship was, trying to hear if more of the raiders were coming.

"I hate being blind like this," he said.

"You think we got all of them?"

"Doubtful."

Caesar twisted around. "Where the hell did 41 go? I've never seen him run from a fight before."

"He didn't," said Kelly, feeling fresh worry welling up. The smoke made him cough. He waved it away from his face and glanced up. "The fire containment chemical hasn't released. We've shorted out something vital."

Caesar slung his die-hard over his shoulder. "I'll see to it," he said and trotted into the mess lounge.

Kelly ran down the corridor to Melaethia's quarters. Instinct made him flatten himself against the wall and approach the door with caution. He hit the chime.

The door slid open, and a percussion shot whined out.

Kelly flinched back. "Hold fire!" he shouted. "It's Kelly!"

"Sorry," replied Beaulieu's voice.

"Coming in now," said Kelly.

"Glad to have you," she said.

Satisfied that she was no longer trigger-happy, Kelly switched off his force shield. He eased himself through the doorway and blinked a moment to let his eyes adjust to the dim light. A barricade of overturned seating had been stretched across half the room. Beaulieu knelt behind it, her dusky face grim and looking every year of her age. She had a stack of torches, her medikit, food packets, blankets, emergency air tanks, and a second percussion pistol with her. Best of all, she had the three wristbands that the children had worn.

Kelly seized these with relief. "Now we can set up some communication lines," he said. "Everyone all right?"

"What's on fire?" asked Beaulieu, climbing stiffly to her feet.

"Circuits. Fire containment isn't working." He looked around a little worriedly. Melaethia and the children weren't in sight. "Where are they?"

Beaulieu glanced toward the rear of the cabin. "Mel?" she called. "All clear."

The door to the head slid open a narrow crack. Kelly glimpsed a pale blur of Melaethia's narrow face.

"Not all clear just yet," he said, nodding his approval of Beaulieu's methods. "We've got them held off . . . for the moment."

"Who the hell are they?" snapped Beaulieu. "Exactly what is going on? What caused that power failure?"

He rubbed his face with his sleeve and when he dropped his arm, Beaulieu was standing by with a sealed pouch of nutritional supplement. He tore it open and swallowed the liquid gratefully. For an instant it was refreshing, then the bitter aftertaste hit the back of his throat and he coughed.

"Salukans," he said, keeping his voice very low although he was sure Melaethia could hear him. "Using Jostics for shock troops. They used some sort of power damping field, but I assume they had to turn it off so their own weapons would work. We're docklinked with them. I don't know yet how many we're up against, but we've thinned them considerably."

"Anyone hurt?"

He shook his head, glad to be able to report that. Beaulieu looked brighter.

"Hey, boss?" said Caesar, poking in his head. "I got the fire put out along this section, but I think it's spreading through the walls."

That was serious indeed. A fire could deplete their oxygen supplies quickly, in addition to the other damage. Fire could never be ignored in space.

Kelly fastened on one of the wristbands and activated the comm. "Kelly to bridge. Come in."

There was a pause, then Siggerson's voice replied cautiously through the blur of the scrambler. He was using maximum distortion, and that probably wasn't good enough against Salukan scanners.

"We've got fire, Siggerson. No containment working from what we can tell."

"Circuit or open?"

Kelly sighed, grateful for Siggerson's calm voice. "Circuit, I'm afraid. Can you monitor its direction?"

" . . . try. Out."

Siggerson was following orders to keep communications short.

Kelly glanced at Caesar. "Keep a watch. They won't wait much longer before they come again."

"Yo." Caesar vanished.

Beaulieu looked at Kelly with worried eyes. "It's been sounding like galactic war out there. How long can we—?"

"I need information," he said in frustration. "I need scanners on that ship—"

"—to count how many are left. Right," she said briskly and turned away from him to sort through her stack of supplies. She pulled out a hand-scanner and passed it to him with a smile. "Limited range, but they couldn't be any closer to us, now, could they?"

Kelly grinned as he took it. "Beaulieu, you're a wonder."

She nodded. "I know. Now sit down while you play with that and let me examine you. You're looking a little blast damaged around the edges."

He shook his head. "No time."

"Commander." She put her hand on his shoulder and glared into his eyes. "We have time. Sit."

5

Saluk, the first mortal, dared enter the Hall of Gods. Of them, he demanded a gift. The gods laughed and dismissed him, but Saluk did not go. Then three immortals gazed upon him with favor. One was Ru, god of the sun, who gave unto Saluk fire. One was Tees, goddess of childbirth, who gave unto Saluk the power to sire children. The last was Choisol, goddess of fate. When she gave him nothing, Saluk feared, thinking she intended to cut his thread of life. But Choisol smiled and said unto him, "Thou hast brought thine own best gift with thee, mortal. Thou hast discovered courage."

—School Manual, general mythology

The secondary ladder well had no lights other than the dim, greenish glow coming off pulsating power feed casings. It was cramped, designed only for occasional maintenance usage, and very hot. 41's shoulders brushed the well on either side, and the very air felt charged with energy waves that crackled lightly upon his skin and made his hair stand out from his head. He felt as though he had entered the guts of a living creature. The pulsing warmth was suffocating, and he had never liked small, enclosed places since his childhood days when Harva Opie had sold him, packed him in a crate, and shipped him into slavery.

He heard the shooting start in the corridor where Kelly and Caesar were fighting. They could handle that end of the job. Now he must do his.

On the tiny landing, he crouched and slipped off his boots, then left them and his die-hard stacked neatly. Snapping open the blades of his prong, he fitted the knife between his teeth and made certain his pistol had a fresh charge pack. He worried about the pistol. Salukans had scanners that detected plasma-energy weapons. It might give him away. But he did not have a percussion weapon with which to replace it.

He moved fast and silently down the ladder. His spine brushed the power feed casing as he descended. He could almost feel the radiation crawling along inside it, yet the casing was well shielded. It was foolish to imagine danger where none existed, but sweat dripped into his eyes, and his breath came short and fast as though he'd been running.

At the bottom of the well, he stepped off the last rung with a deep sigh and wiped his mouth with a palm that tasted of the metal he'd been grasping. A low growl from the shadows to his left startled him.

His eyes searched fast, and he spied Ouoji crouched near a conduit hole, watching what was happening on the other side of the wall. 41 dropped down beside her, his face close enough to be brushed by the silky tips of her fur as he also peered through the crack.

One Jostic in half armor, guarding the airlock. One Salukan, shimmering in his force belt, pacing with his head tilted to listen to the sounds of fighting on deck two.

There came the roar of an explosion that shook the ship. The Salukan curled and ducked through the airlock.

It was time.

41 uncoiled his body and stepped close to the hatch that so far had kept the enemy from discovering this ladder. He must be quick. He must appear and kill the sentry before anyone discovered where he had come from. He must move . . . *now*.

He used the knife, because it could be thrown silently. The weapon hit its mark in the Jostic's eye.

Even as the creature arched back in agony, hands to its face, 41 was scooting through the hatch, shoving it closed, and running.

He yanked the prong from the Jostic's eye socket, spilling gore, and struck again in another, more vulnerable spot before the Jostic could scream a warning.

The sentry fell dead at 41's feet. He heard silence, marred only by his own panting, and exchanged the bloodied prong for his pistol. Ducking into the airlock, he inhaled the mingled stenches of death, carbonite, slagged metal, and filthy air emanating from the ship beyond the link.

Fear hit him unexpectedly. He would die in there, and the Jostic savages would eat his remains.

The fear—a legacy from his imprisonment among the cyborgs of Methanus—shamed him. It made the insides of his belly coil like hot liquid. But even as he hesitated, 41 knew that surrendering to fear would only make it worse. He would rather die than be eaten away from the inside.

Baring his teeth, 41 ran forward.

His only chance was to be quick. He would have to go in shooting and try to destroy some of the ship's piloting controls if possible. As he ran across the soft tunnel forming the link, a fist seemed to keep clutching his insides, and his mind was broken with distracting thoughts and images.

Kevalyn, gray-eyed and beautiful . . . Kelly, her brother and his friend . . . Melaethia, she-devil temptress who made him ache in strange ways . . . He whipped through the open airlock on the other side and fired pointblank into the guts of a surprised Jostic pilot.

The pilot screamed as he fell, bringing the four other occupants of the bridge around. 41 dropped to one knee and cut a swath of vicious fire even as his mind noted that this ship was of old Salukan make, with its airlock at the top near the bridge area, and was not well maintained. The overhead lights were dimmed to battle-action intensity. Their black suits made the Jostics hard to see as they yelled and dived for cover.

Both percussion bullets and plasma bolts came back at him. 41 rolled and took cover behind the pilot's console, using the dead body as a partial shield. He needed to shift position fast, keep all of his opponents to one side of him and not let them circle behind him, but at the moment damaging the ship was more important than saving himself.

The dead pilot wore a key on a long chain about his neck. 41 snapped the chain and fitted the key into a small notch at the base of the console. It was difficult to fire and keep his head down and open the base all at the same time. 41 knew he was missing too many shots. He heard a Jostic dart behind him. Breaking cover, 41 reared up and shot the man, who reeled over backwards with a hoarse scream.

A bullet singed 41 across the skull; another struck him in the back of the thigh. He fell, half-blinded with blood that gushed across his vision. His leg felt as though it had been kicked. It was numb, useless, unable to support him. He groped blindly upon the cushioned deck, a small corner of his brain registering the filth of accumulated dirt and food particles which layered the floor.

The Jostics grunted to each other in their feeble language. They were cautious with him, not emerging from cover for several seconds. That gave 41 time to drag himself around until he could grasp the key and turn it. His hand had dark amber blood on it—his blood. He could only see through his right eye, and there was a mighty pounding in his head, growing louder with every heartbeat. He felt the urgency of too little time, of seconds fleeing from him into the stream of missed opportunities. When he rolled onto his side, the pressure on his leg let air into the wound and agony rammed into his body.

"Shevul drive all of you into the void!" shouted a hoarse, angry voice in Saluk. "Fools! I leave you for an instant, and what have you let destroy the flight deck? Where is the pilot?"

"*Huh, huh, huh,*" snuffled one of the Jostics. "Pilot dead. Intruder dead."

Angry footsteps came his way. 41 resisted the need to rest. His one good eye wanted to close. His leg felt like it was being twisted off by a set of gigantic pincers. But he needed to finish first. He grasped the panel and pushed it open. His hand felt a million parsecs away.

"Do you think, in that dim skull of yours, that you have accomplished something?" continued the hoarse Salukan. "If the pilot is dead, who will fly us home? Who?"

41 stared at the bewildering blur of complicated circuitry. He should stick his fingers into it and pull out those delicate filaments. But his fingers slid to the deck and lay there. The pounding in his head got louder, until even the angry voices coming closer were not of importance.

"Humans have pilot," said the Jostic sullenly.

"But you have not yet taken the Earthers *or* their ship," said the Salukan. "By the time you are finished, that ship will be destroyed, and we need it to—"

"*Our* salvage!" said the Jostic angrily. "*Ours*!"

In their argument, they stopped on the other side of the console. 41 could not see them except for the Salukan's heel. 41 lifted his pistol a fraction, trying to aim it at the circuits. The two muzzles wavered. He could feel strength ebbing from his fingers, but he struggled to finish this task Kelly had asked of him.

He . . . must not . . . fail . . . Kelly.

"Enough!" said the Salukan. "They will retaliate soon. I am throwing the damping field before they—"

41 squeezed the trigger, and plasma flashed into the guts of the astrogation, steering, propulsion, and stabilizer controls, fusing the circuits into a solid, ruined mass. The backlash scorched 41's hand, but he no longer felt it, no longer heard the cries of outrage, no longer saw the effect he had created.

41 dropped into darkness, and knew nothing more.

Up on deck two of the *Sabre*, Kelly finished scanning the enemy ship. The life signs kept wavering. He thought he'd detected five Jostics, then four, then two. There were perhaps three or four Salukans as well. One of them could be 41, if he had somehow gained access to the ship. Kelly frowned in worry, but forced himself to keep planning. 41 could take care of himself.

Kelly called Siggerson. "Bridge, any luck in breaking that tractor?"

"Negative."

"Any progress?"

"Negative."

Siggerson could be a bit more informative than that, Kelly thought.

Phila called back. "Sir, fire is contained."

"Good. We're going to start a—"

She broke the line. Frowning, Kelly found himself talking to thin air. He punched the comm angrily, but nothing reactivated. The lights in Melaethia's quarters and the corridor beyond went out.

"Oh, *hell*!" said Kelly in alarm. "Everyone, grab something!"

Just as he spoke, gravity failed, and he went floating toward the ceiling. There was nothing he could do but relax until his head bumped gently. He grabbed a rung in the darkness, and oriented himself toward the door.

"Beaulieu," he said. "Are you fixed?"

"Yes," she said crisply as though this was nothing more than a null-gravity drill. "I'm about two and a half meters from you, in a diagonal away from the door."

"Right. Melaethia?"

It took the Salukan woman a few seconds to reply. Her voice was low with agitation. "I am . . . I am near the floor. I have the table in my hands. My children—"

Kelly heard them crying. He said quickly, "Don't try to go to them yet. Orient yourself first."

"How?"

"Wait," said Beaulieu before Kelly could start explaining. "I have some solid combustible bricks in my supplies. Let me find them."

"Make it fast," he said, keeping one ear attuned toward the corridor. "They're going to pull something any minute."

In the darkness, floating, the waiting seemed endless. In reality Beaulieu took no more than two minutes to propel herself to the floor, find her supply stash on the floor and strike-ignite one of the fuel bricks.

It blazed up, white light creating stark shadows in the corners of the room. Melaethia gasped, muttering something in Saluk, and attempted to swim toward the head. All that did was spin her helplessly end over end until she bumped into a wall.

"I'll help her," said Beaulieu before Kelly could go to her aid. "Take these."

She tossed the percussion pistols his way. The weapons floated at a graceful angle until they lost impetus, then they began spinning. Kelly launched himself toward them from the ceiling, making sure his angle would carry him on toward the door. He got it right, passing them close enough to grab them without bobbling his trajectory.

Caesar appeared in the doorway, however, and blocked him from making a perfect exit. Kelly bounced back into the room, but Caesar grabbed his sleeve and pulled him into the corridor.

They floated, almost nose to nose, and Kelly handed him one of the pistols. "Use this and your prong," he said. "Drop the plasma weapons."

In the backwash of light spilling out from Melaethia's quarters, Caesar had lost all color and was only a combination of pale and dark shadows. He nodded, folded stock and muzzle of his die-hard, and released it.

"Boss," said Caesar in a low voice, "we can't defend this deck, not with these pop guns and a couple of prongs. How much air do we have if they keep life support shut down?"

"We've used up most of it," estimated Kelly with a frown. "The fire didn't help. Maybe half an hour."

"You think 41 made it to their ship?"

The question hung between them. Kelly looked into Caesar's eyes and didn't answer. He didn't have to. They both knew that even if 41 had bought them a few extra minutes of time, it wasn't really going to help. Kelly fought off a feeling of resignation. That wasn't going to help either.

"Well, we don't have much firepower, but then neither do they," he said, keeping his voice firm. "This damned field they're using works both ways."

"Hand-to-hand with a Jostic is no fun," muttered Caesar. "And whatever you do, don't let them get one of those screamers stuck to your hide. Red-hot needles in your nervous system is nothing like it."

"I know," said Kelly. He glanced up and down the corridor, getting edgy now as they waited. So far he'd heard nothing from either ladder well. The damaged lift remained dead, its doors open like a mouth. "They can take us from one side or both, if they've discovered the second ladder."

"We need a fall-back plan," said Caesar. "The bridge and arsenal stores are our last—"

"No," said Kelly grimly. "I'm not taking the battle up to the bridge. We'll hold them here."

"But, boss!"

"We'll hold them here as long as we can. After that, Mohatsa has her orders."

Caesar's eyes widened. Kelly heard the quick rasp of his breath. "Destruct?" he whispered.

Fear raked one claw down the wall of Kelly's own intentions. He shivered, but held firm. "There's no other way."

"There's survival!" said Caesar.

"For some of us, perhaps," said Kelly in a voice like iron. "But this ship doesn't fall into Salukan hands. You *know* that!"

"Yeah, I know it," muttered Caesar. "But, hell, you making Phila do it? You think she's got the guts?"

"Better up there, than down here being shock fodder."

Caesar's hand slapped his shoulder, driving him into the wall. "Oh, no, it's not. She's not officer trained. You can't put that responsibility on her. She'll crack. It's *your* job, Bryan. Siggerson won't blow the ship. He'd die first."

Kelly frowned, angry with Caesar's interference, but knowing he was right. Phila was their youngest. She was gutsy and tough, and she'd seasoned into a capable operative. But she didn't handle major responsibility stress well. She would never make it to command. It was his job to blow them all to bits, if the time came, not hers.

"You'd think," said Caesar, trying to make a joke, "that they'd ask us to surrender."

Kelly wasn't in the mood for jokes, even now. He shifted his hold on a rung to get the right launch angle. It was going to be tough finding his way in the dark.

"They should be coming by now," he said uneasily. "I don't like this. They're up to some trick."

"Or waiting for us to make the first stupid move," said Caesar. "Boss, I—"

"Forget it. You're right," said Kelly. "I'm going now to send Phila down here. If 41 comes back—"

"Yeah."

Neither of them believed that. Not now. He'd been gone too long.

Kelly kicked himself off, using his momentum well, making sure he didn't bobble off course when he floated beyond the reach of light. The darkness was almost a palpable thing, and the cold air smelled dangerously stale.

His lungs caught, but it was only nervousness. He'd know the difference when the air really began to run out. The

environmental suits were stored in lockers on the third deck.
No way to get at them now.

The regrets always came, if you had time enough. The
political analysts had guessed wrong about the Salukans
wanting Melaethia back. They wanted her and her children
dead. Kelly and his squad had been dispatched just a few hours
too late to avoid this assassination team. Well, they would all
die together if they had to. And the information branch of
Allied Intelligence would make sure the whole galaxy knew
that Salukans had ruthlessly slaughtered a young mother and
her defenseless children.

He fumbled his way into the ladder well and climbed until at
last his outstretched fingers found the open hatch leading into
the bridge. It was supposed to be sealed. His sense of
uneasiness grew. What were the Jostics waiting on? What were
they up to?

As soon as he floated inside, he had his answers. He saw a
dim blue light shining off the top of a small canister near the
viewscreen. Siggerson and Mohatsa were floating unconscious
or dead near their respective stations. There was a steady
hissing sound and the sharp, pungent smell of oranges and sour
milk.

Alarms went off inside Kelly. Holding his breath, he tried to
retreat, but it was too late. Already he could feel his hands and
feet going numb. The bridge swam in his vision and his
slackened body tumbled in a loose spin.

He could not close the hatch to keep the gas from escaping
into the rest of the ship. He could not even wonder how the hell
the canister had gotten up here. It was too late to wonder . . .
too late . . .

6

Beware the chains of kinship. Guard thy honor first.
—maxim of Rienjeth II

Wearing a mask although all traces of the gas had been flushed from the ventilation systems of the Earther ship, Dausal limped along the scarred, blackened corridor in the glare of temporary lights rigged up to replace those destroyed in the battle. The light hurt his eyes despite the goggles he wore. He cursed it as he cursed these stubborn Earthers who had made everything so difficult.

It was a great piece of interference on their part to keep the rightful Pharaon from his throne. That they were willing to die for that purpose made this a blood-vengeance between the Empire and the Alliance. Dausal's lips tightened in satisfaction. He would enjoy leading that war. It would make up for many wrongs.

His boots crunched upon a litter of broken glass and plastics within the dispensary. Melaethia and the children had been revived within the inner treatment room. They remained there now, guarded by two of the Jostics, who gave him sloppy salutes as he entered.

Melaethia looked up at the sound of the door sliding shut

behind him. Her eyes widened, and the color drained from her face, leaving it a sickly yellow hue.

He stopped three strides from her and let himself look at her, this sister of his blood, this creature that he hated. She wore her hair like a tribeless female. That was fitting, but her conformity to custom, even in matters of shame, angered him. He fed on the hate a moment, savoring its heat in his veins. Nothing, he made sure, changed in his face.

Slowly he removed his goggles and mask. The light in here was muted, soft, but it took effort not to squint. *I am nearly blind because of you.* He wanted to savage her, and the effort to stop that swift rush of fury became a painful one. But mastering himself brought a sort of pleasure too.

She rose from the bed where the three children slept. Her eyes, so beautifully shaped, stared at him with the blankness of non-recognition. He said nothing, just went on staring, while color returned in a slow, bronze tide to her cheeks. Her chin went up with a haughtiness he found pathetic. Was she remembering her days as a concubine, when no man was allowed to see her splendid face?

"The humiliations are just beginning, *masere* of the people's heart." His ruined voice was a hoarse rasp of malevolence.

She flinched. "My son is not Pharaon yet."

"They will honor your womb for its sacred contents, but no one has forgotten your crimes, Masere."

"Don't call me that!"

He took half a step closer and watched her fight the urge to shrink back. "Masere will be your title, Mother of Pharaon."

"No!" But she whispered the word. Her eyes shimmered with horror and fear.

He found it delicious.

"Who *are* you?" she asked.

The rage returned, beating inside him like a winged insect attacking a light. To govern himself he turned and bent over the sleeping children. They lay tumbled together in innocence. Their small faces were worn with fatigue.

First battle. He wondered if they had tasted Earther blood yet. He wondered if he dared give any to them. His scarred, blue-stained fingertip reached out to gently touch one small cheek. The skin was so tender, the color of new honey. His emotions shifted, and suddenly he wanted to weep over these little ones, who had brought him back to life.

"D-Dausal?" said Melaethia.

The emotions in her voice made him jerk away from the children. He glared at her, his skin feeling suddenly too small for his bones. She was at the peak of her womanhood. Her beauty had increased twofold. Her skin and eyes glowed with health. He could smell her fertility, like something ripe and beckoning beneath the barriers she had up. And what did she see in him now, her once handsome brother? Why did her eyes dig at his face as though she could not be certain of her own guess? He saw the skin tighten around her eyes, saw the frown, the hint of pity and distaste.

"I am Dausal," he said hoarsely.

With a cry, she came to him in a rush, and when her hands closed upon his shoulders, he struck her a backhanded blow that sent her reeling to the floor. The sound cracked between them and echoed in the silence afterwards. On the bed, the male child sat up, suddenly awake, his eyes like obsidian. He drew back his small lips and hissed a warning.

Dausal ignored him. Melaethia huddled on the floor for a few moments, then slowly pushed herself upright and turned to face him. He could see the mark of his hand upon her skin. It pleased him.

"What do you see?" he said to her. "A monster? How do you like my crookedness, dear sister? How do you like my shortened leg? Do you want to see all my scars? See my hands? See where some of the fingers have been broken more than once?"

"Dausal, *please*—"

"What do you beg for? Your life?"

She pressed her hands to her mouth. "Your forgiveness," she said, but the words were muffled and he did not believe them.

He lost interest in her and eyed the boy, who was still watching. "He is not trained."

"No."

"That is good. The chancellors hoped it would be in their hands."

"He is not Pharaon! He will not be trained into a—"

Dausal struck her again, not as hard this time, but it was enough to make her bend over with shudders of grief. The boy hissed again, more loudly, and succeeded in waking his sisters.

Dausal whirled on them all. "*Aret!*" he snapped, using the command tone although it was forbidden.

The boy sank down on his small haunches, his face puckered. One of the girls began to snivel.

"What have they promised you for this, Dausal?" asked Melaethia angrily. "Did they promise to make you regent? You, a father-killer?"

"I did not kill him!" shouted Dausal. "His own—"

"You betrayed him, betrayed your own father!" she shouted back. "If the Earthers had been less clever, he would have died before he could escape. What is worse than a son who turns on his own sire? Your heart is black and your soul is dead! You will surely perish in—"

"Silence!" roared Dausal.

She stood cowed, her head bent, her nostrils flaring with each rapid breath. He glared at her, wanting to choke the defiance from her. How dare she show no shame? How dare she throw accusations at him? She and Arnaht had shaken the very foundations of the Empire, but Dausal had paid for it.

Her time, however, would come—and come soon. He waited until he could control his breathing again.

"You are going to Gamael," he said. "You will stand upon the steps of the Temple Hall of Justice and you will beg for your life. You will beg for your blood. You will beg for the mercy of the people. You will walk naked, on your knees, from there to the inner Court. Twelve citizens of the Houses will stone you. If you live, you will be permitted to exist within the Defended City. You will be called Masere, and you will wear veils encrusted in gold. But you will live alone, with only mute eunuchs and handmaidens to serve you. You will live within walls, where none may see you. No voice will speak to you. No company will come to entertain you with court gossip and chatter. Once a year, upon the occasion of the Pharaon's birthday, you will be permitted to attend the festival in gracious robes at the side of your son's throne. But during this honor you will not speak and no one will speak directly to you. That is your sentence, killer of Nefir. That is the rest of your life, traitoress."

He took great satisfaction in saying those words to her, in watching the spirit drain from her graceful form, in watching her eyes go wide in fear. He wanted her to seek his intervention. He wanted her to plead for his influence in gaining her a kinder sentence. He wanted to hold her sanity in his hands and let her quiver on the whim of his decision.

But she did not kneel and she did not beg. She stared at him as though her face were frozen. Then she said, "You have become a twisted, piteous thing, Dausal. I warned you not to betray our father. I told you that it would eat you from within, and it has. I take no pleasure in being right. And whatever you want from me now, as you gloat and insult me, I shall not give it to you. I shall defy you and spit upon your honor until one of us breathes no more. Now get out of here and leave us be!"

He saw the look in her eyes, the same look in all their eyes, all four of them staring at him with pity and disgust. The rage thudded inside him until he thought his eyes would explode from the pressure. He raised his fists at her, but he did not strike out again. Afraid he could no longer control himself, he turned and limped from the dispensary, seething with resentment that she had guessed he had little authority. She would pay for that as well, he vowed. She must.

"Dausal."

He came up short in the corridor and waited for the slim, elegant minlord to catch up with him.

Segatha was of Toth House on both sides. His shaven skull was as narrow as Dausal's hand, his breeding perfect in every line. Even now, although the Earthers had all been captured, he still wore his force belt. It shimmered in a golden nimbus about his person.

"All the possible repairs have been performed. The Jostic ship will not function properly."

"It must," said Dausal in alarm. "Are you certain they are not lying? They are lazy, these Jostics. They want—"

"We have propulsion, but steering and stabilizers are hope-lessly fused," said Segatha patiently, although his golden eyes flicked to Dausal's face and away. "I have suggested taking parts from this ship, but the technologies are not compatible and the parts cannot be interchanged. Shall I revive the Earther pilot and—"

"No! We do not need Earther assistance."

Segatha frowned. "Then we must abandon our ship and use this one."

"No!"

"Dausal, it is the only way! The damage to this ship is minimal. Nothing in its essential operation has been injured. We intended to take it with us anyway. Why not—"

"Because we won't go home in an enemy ship as though we lost our own!" said Dausal angrily. "That is to shame us."

"There is no shame in bringing home a ship of the StarHawks," said Segatha. "There is no shame in having six Hawks as prisoners to place under the mind sieve. There is no shame in having our Pharaon safe in Salukan hands once again. We have accomplished much."

His words blurred in Dausal's mind.

"Dausal," said Segatha with an edge to his voice, "heed me. We have not much time until other ships come looking. They launched a log buoy, and they sent a message for help. We must go soon. We must use this ship. Destroy that Jostic wreck so that the Alliance will have no proof of our being in their space. Let us not lose our advantage now."

Dausal jerked his shoulders and started on down the corridor, refusing to meet Segatha's eyes. Segatha pretended to defer to him in everything but addressed rank, but he knew that Segatha secretly scorned him.

"Have it be so," he said without glancing back. "And hurry. Hurry!"

The sharp scent of something chemical and bitter went up Kelly's nostrils and jolted his brain awake. Startled, he sneezed and opened his eyes, shifting his head away from the smell.

Before he was fully focused, however, a rough hand seized him and pulled him onto his feet. "*Hut!*" said a voice in Saluk.

Kelly found himself staring at the tan imperial uniform, wig, and leather cheek straps of a Salukan trooper. The man's eyes blazed with impatience. He gave Kelly another shake and slapped him so hard Kelly's head rang from the blow.

He shifted his jaw gingerly, thinking for a brief moment that it might be broken. But when he looked up again, he was fully alert and mad.

The trooper stepped back, holding a blaster trained on Kelly. An officer wearing a blue sash worked in symbols of the Toth House rather than the imperial seal walked up. His oiled skull gleamed in the dim lights overhead. His eyes were keen and intelligent.

"State your name," he said in fluent Glish, almost without accent.

"Kelly."

"Rank?"

"Commander."

"You are StarHawks."

Kelly paused a moment, judging the man. "Yes, Special Operations."

"You are not the pilot," said the officer. He glanced around the lounge, where the tables had been overturned and shoved up against one wall. The rest of Kelly's squad lay unconscious on the floor where they had apparently been dumped. Kelly frowned at them in concern, but with the trooper guarding him like a tensed coil, he dared not move. "Which is the pilot?"

"Why?"

The trooper stepped forward to strike Kelly, but the officer interceded.

"Your life is a very feeble thread with us," said the officer. "Don't be foolish. Three of you were found on the bridge. Another man and one of your females? Which is the pilot?"

Kelly's brows went up. "That should be obvious. Salukans don't believe women are intelligent."

"You are incorrect," said the officer stiffly. "We know the Alliance uses females in combat situations. Because we disapprove does not mean we fail to understand."

Kelly bowed his head slightly. "Touché."

"I do not ask again. Chuteph!"

The trooper swung his blaster around and trained it upon the back of Beaulieu's head. She was lying on her stomach, sprawled like a doll which has been dropped, vulnerable. Kelly frowned, aware that the Salukans were capable of killing in cold blood.

He pointed at Siggerson.

"Good." The officer gestured and Chuteph went to snap a vial under Siggerson's nostrils and shake him into consciousness. "This is a sophisticated ship. How many are required to operate her?"

Kelly dared not underestimate the officer's knowledge. "Two," he said.

"Ah." The officer's gaze flickered. "I am Minlord Segatha. You and your pilot will make checks to be sure there is no damage we have overlooked. Then I shall give you the course heading we are to take."

"Why not keep us on tractor beam?" said Kelly. "It will mess up our photonic drive, but that won't matter once we're scrapped for parts."

Segatha's lips tightened briefly in what could have been a smile. "We prefer to follow the decision we have made. Move. Now."

He pointed at the door and Kelly started for it. Siggerson stumbled along after him, with the two Salukans bringing up the rear. Kelly could not help glancing back at the rest of his squad in concern.

"How long will they be unconscious?"

"Until they are revived," said Segatha. "It is a kind of nerve paralysis and requires a precise counter-agent."

"Some of them may need medical attention—"

"It does not matter," said Segatha. "We have other tasks. Move."

Kelly and Siggerson exchanged a look and started down the corridor past the ruined lift to the ladder well. They went up, through the bridge, and into the rest of deck one. The arsenal, Kelly noted with regret as he glanced through the half-opened door, had been emptied. The battery room hummed, everything in perfect order, all green on every systems check.

"Have you seen Ouoji?" whispered Siggerson as he bent over the reserve battery panel.

"No—"

"Who is Ouoji?" demanded Segatha sharply. "Hawk squads are six in complement. Who is Ouoji?"

"Our ship's mascot," said Kelly, irritated by his paranoia. "A pet."

"Pet?" Segatha looked blank a moment as though the word wasn't in his vocabulary. Then he blinked and frowned at Chuteph. "Pass the word. When it is found, have it killed."

Siggerson straightened with a jerk. Crimson stained his face. "You damned—"

Kelly caught him before he could rush at Segatha. Siggerson fought him, but Kelly pinned him against the wall.

"They can't kill her!" said Siggerson desperately. "She isn't any harm to them. They can't—"

"Siggerson!" said Kelly, determined to calm him before Chuteph used more brutal methods. "There isn't anything we can do. Siggerson!"

Slowly the tension slackened in Siggerson's thin body. His shoulders slumped and he looked at Kelly with such naked appeal Kelly had to drop his own gaze.

"She's just a little animal," said Siggerson, his voice pleading. "No harm to anyone. Kelly, don't let them—"

"Perhaps they won't find her," said Kelly, aware that the Jostics would eat her if they got the chance. He tried not to think about it.

"This man is a fool," said Segatha with scorn. "Does a pet mean more to him than his own life?"

"Do you have children?" retorted Kelly. "Do you love them?"

Segatha looked blank. "I do not understand."

"Never mind," said Kelly with scorn of his own. "It's useless to explain."

Segatha caught the scorn, and the expression in his eyes flattened into something more hostile than he'd previously exhibited. "Finish your work," he said.

"Everything checks out," said Kelly.

Segatha stood to one side and pointed back the way they'd

come. "To the bridge. The coordinates are waiting in the astrogation computer."

"You entered them?" said Siggerson.

"Do you think we cannot understand your technology?" Segatha sneered. "You Earthers give yourselves much false pride. Take the given heading and go to distort speed 9."

Siggerson started back to the bridge but Kelly hesitated. "Why not kill us now and dump us out?" he said. "It's going to be difficult guarding us all the way back to Gamael."

"Why do you think we are going to Gamael?"

Kelly met his gaze squarely. "Do you think we cannot understand your politics?"

Segatha's cheeks darkened. "What was the word you used? Touché? A fencing term. I understand the reference."

"So why not dispose of us here?"

"And leave bodies to be found?" said Segatha in a mocking tone. "There will be nothing found. And the Minzanese who come in response to your distress call will not search hard."

He paused a moment, then added, "We have tracked your log buoy and destroyed it."

Kelly managed to swallow his emotions on that one, but just as he reached the bridge there came a slight shudder through the ship. On the viewscreen he saw an explosion flare. Hope rushed into his throat. He thought for a moment that rescue had come, no matter how improbably, and had fired on the Jostic ship.

"Let them play with that debris," said Segatha with a chuckle. "Jostic filth and rubbish, nothing more."

Hope plummetted in Kelly so fast he felt a surge of corresponding lightheadedness. Only then did he become aware of the lingering aftereffects of the gas: a numb sort of tingling in his extremities, a faint sensation of imminent nausea, a rawness in his lungs as though he'd inhaled water.

"So 41 did damage your ship," he said aloud. "And you have to use ours to get home. Careless of you."

Segatha swung around to meet his gaze. "Nevertheless, Kelly, we are the victors here. Get to your post."

7

To hunt well, know when to attack and when to lie in wait.

—Saluk proverb

After jump was safely made, and the *Sabre* was set at a cruising speed of TD 9, Segatha ordered everything set upon full automateds and dismissed Kelly and Siggerson from the bridge. Siggerson tried to protest, but the Jostic guards hit him, and after that he gave no more trouble as they were hustled down to deck two and left there.

Surprised at being released, Kelly left Siggerson, who still looked shaken, and did some exploration. He found the hatch to the emergency ladder had been crudely welded shut. A Jostic stood on guard in the main ladder well. That left them prisoners; contained, but not in need of close supervision.

Although the whole situation made Kelly seethe with frustration, he was grateful that they had some freedom. That gave them a chance, however slim, to figure out a way to escape this mess.

Returning to the lounge, he found that the others had all been revived. Melaethia and the children weren't in sight. He hoped they were being held separately and had not already been executed. Caesar and Phila looked groggy, but all right.

Beaulieu, however, had 41 sitting on one of the tables and was grimly digging a bullet out of his leg.

Kelly went over to watch. The light was poor in here for surgery, but Beaulieu was wearing her surgical goggles. 41, his face stained with dried blood from a nasty gash over one eye, sat quietly, his trouser leg slit open to above his knee. He glanced at Kelly, but did not speak. Despite the number of anesthetic patches around the wound, he flinched when Beaulieu dug too hard.

She swore and tossed down her probe for another one. "Not so close, Kelly. I don't have a sterilization field going, and this is bad enough."

Kelly frowned in concern. It looked more like butchery than surgery. 41 was very pale at the mouth. "Why aren't you in sickbay, doing this properly?"

Beaulieu glared at him through the goggles. Before she could answer, Kelly grimaced in apology.

"Sorry, Doctor. I didn't mean it quite that way."

"Those damned brutes won't let me use it," she said angrily. "All I can have is my field medikit, and I had to damned near fight them for that. Idiotic baboons, they must have three brain cells among the lot. There's not even blood plasma for—"

"Beaulieu," said 41 in a strained voice.

She looked at him sharply and plucked off one of the patches that had turned dark blue on top to show that its dosage had expired. "Hold this," she said to Kelly, and slapped it into his palm. "41, I don't think you should have any more localized. Can you stand five more minutes?"

41 nodded. Beaulieu went back to work. This time when 41 flinched, Kelly put a quick hand on his shoulder. 41's muscles were roped up tight. Perspiration had soaked his hairline.

"Well, 41," said Kelly, keeping his own voice steady, "when I expressed a wish that we could take out the Jostics' ship, I didn't mean for you to take yourself out with them."

A flicker of something close to shame passed through 41's eyes. "Didn't do enough . . . damage," he said. "*Darshon!*"

"Sorry," said Beaulieu and held up the bullet in her forceps. "There it is. It tumbled when it hit, making minced meat of you, then lodged against the bone where it didn't want to come out. Hold him, Kelly. This will sting a bit."

She sprayed something into the wound. Kelly gripped both of 41's shoulders, feeling a queasy turn in his own stomach. Beaulieu sealed the wound neatly and sprayed on a dressing. Then she went to work on 41's forehead. With that wound disinfected and sealed, she stripped off her goggles and blinked at 41 critically.

"Holding?" she said.

He nodded.

"Still hurt?"

"Not so much," said 41. His eyes shifted to Kelly, who smiled.

"You did plenty of damage. They had to abandon their own ship and they're using ours. That gives us a chance to get them yet."

41 grunted. "You will still destroy us?"

"No, not now."

"Why not?"

"Because there's no one on board, with the possible exception of the minlord, who really knows what he's looking at. And because I intend to regain control of the *Sabre* long before we reach Gamael."

41 nodded, apparently satisfied. "I would rather not fight in order to destroy ourselves."

Kelly had to smile. "No, you would rather pull a heroic stunt and get yourself shot full of holes."

"There is a difference, Kelly."

"I know."

"Caesar," said Beaulieu, "come over and lend a hand. 41 needs some rest."

Caesar obliged and with 41 between him and Kelly they maneuvered him off the table and onto his good foot, taking care not to jar him too much.

"To your cabin?" asked Kelly.

"The cabins are sealed," said Caesar. "We have the mess lounge and the corridor to play in. Anything else we want, we have to ask permission."

Kelly frowned, thinking of weapons stashed in his quarters. Segatha was more clever than he'd thought.

"There," said 41, pointing.

They got him to the corner and lowered him gently to the floor. Phila tossed over a blanket, and Kelly tucked it around him while 41 scooted back to prop his shoulders against the wall. Beaulieu came to stare at him a moment, her lips pursed thoughtfully.

"How long until he's functional?" said Kelly.

"He needs to stay off that leg a full five days," she said. "Without our re-gen facilities, it will be slow to heal and—"

"We have twenty-eight solar days to Gamael," said Kelly. "Ten before we enter Salukan space. I want us to make our move before then."

Caesar rubbed his thatch of red hair. "If we can figure out how to get into the arsenal—"

"Forget it," said Kelly. "They've emptied it."

"Everything?" said Caesar in dismay.

"I wasn't allowed to stop and look, but, yes, it looks bare."

Phila glanced at Siggerson. "Do you think we could tap into auxiliary through the circuitry? Hey, Siggerson! I'm talking to you."

Siggerson glanced up. He looked worried and upset. "The circuitry? Uh, no, doubt it. Fused."

"Maybe not all of it," said Phila.

Kelly nodded at her. "First try to rig up some means of telling when they're scanning us. I'd like us to be clear of surveillance in here."

She grinned and winked. "Hokay, sir. One snoop alarm coming up. Then I start checking what's fused and what's not. You going to help, Siggerson?"

He looked at her reluctantly. "What about Ouoji? We need to look for her."

"No," said Kelly. "I have a feeling Ouoji can take care of herself. If we find her, then they find her. Leave her be for now, Siggerson. Help Phila."

Siggerson got to his feet and cast a look around at all of them. "Do any of you really believe we stand a chance? Why should the Salukans even bother with taking us all the way to

Gamael? You know what they do to prisoners. We're unimportant to them now that they've got our ship and Melaethia. They'll dump us before—"

"Shut up!" said Caesar, lifting his fists. "Just shut up! You've got the guts of a gubworm, you know that? Did it ever occur to you, while you're so busy whining, that they have to keep *you* alive? You're the one that knows how to handle the ship. So since you're pretty much guaranteed not to be dumped before we reach Gamael, you might have the decency not to remind the rest of us just how expendable we are."

There was an appalled silence when Caesar finished.

Siggerson blinked at them, his face pale. "I apologize," he said at last. "I—I guess I wasn't thinking clearly. I didn't mean to imply—"

"Aw, go stuff yourself," said Caesar in disgust. "Okay if I go prowl, boss?"

"Yes," said Kelly.

Siggerson's gaze went to Kelly. "I didn't—"

"We know," said Kelly gently, aware that all of them were under a strain, aware that the strain would only get worse. "Why don't you see about helping Phila now?"

Siggerson nodded and shuffled after Mohatsa, who shot him a scornful glance but let him help her open up a circuit panel.

Kelly's and Beaulieu's eyes met. He sighed.

"He's not trained for this kind of pressure," said Beaulieu.

"I know."

"What do you want me to do?" asked Beaulieu.

"Take account of the food stores. Do you know if the Salukans are going to use our rations or theirs?"

"Theirs, I imagine," she said. "I suspect they're feeding the Jostics a substance to keep them under control."

He nodded, relieved. "What about this gas we've all breathed? Any long-term adverse effects?"

"Not if they don't use it again," she said. "I'm not sure what it was. But I'm never very happy about nerve gas, however mild. You're right. Everyone will do better once they've eaten."

"Good," said Kelly. "I'm going to talk to Melaethia."

"You think they'll let you?"

"I'm about to find out."

* * *

The Jostic guarding the ladder well was not in sight when Kelly stepped into the corridor. He went to Melaethia's quarters and buzzed for admittance.

"Go away," she said in Saluk. "I do not receive you."

"Melaethia, it's Kelly. May I speak with you?"

She took so long to reply he thought she'd refused, but at last her door slid open. She faced him with a mixture of anger and something he couldn't read. She looked slender, almost child-like, in the shapeless houserobe she wore. Her hair was tangled. She stood in the doorway as though she did not mean to let him enter.

"Why speak to me?" she said in Glish. "I am in shame. I do not—"

"It's important," he said. "Please."

She frowned, but she stepped aside. Kelly entered quickly and felt relieved when the door shut.

"I wasn't sure if they weren't keeping you apart from us for some reason—"

"I am not a prisoner," she said proudly.

"Then it's better if you stay with us," he said.

"No."

"Melaethia—"

"No!" She made a slashing gesture with her hand. "I am in shame. Do you have no understanding?"

"No, I do not understand. Shame because they're taking you back to Gamael?"

She laughed. "If that were only all. Kelly, you are not kinsman. You and your squad are strangers. To me, there is no tie, not for blood and not for dying."

"Humans believe that ties can come from compassion and a sense of justice as much as from kinship."

"No! Your people have died for us, died for my son. It is not right. We—"

"Melaethia, no one has died," he said gently.

"I have smelled the blood. Lying does not become a man of your rank."

"41 was shot. The rest of us are bruised and nicked, but no one is dead," he said. "Come and see if you don't believe me."

Her eyes widened and a stillness came over her. "41?"

"It's not serious. We're going to eat soon. We would like you to join us."

Gladness, relief, and shyness raced through her eyes. She drew back and turned half away.

"You have to eat," he said.

"Food is not important. I am the cause of this trouble."

"Vanity will be your downfall, Melaethia," he said, laughing. "This trouble has been going on as long as humans and Salukans have known each other. You're just a small part of it."

"You have been fighting battle and you have no anger," she said in wonderment. "Truly Earthers are strange."

"Truly we are," he said with a smile. "And I'm angry all right, but not at you. We blundered and let them catch us flat-footed. I intend to find out about that damping field they have, if possible. And we have many plans to lay. I'd rather you were present to hear them the first time."

"Plans?"

"For retaking the ship. You don't think I mean to let Segatha get away with this, do you?"

Again the stillness came over her. She regarded Kelly for several seconds. "There is in you much heart. The Minzanese lack this."

"I suppose they do. That's why we've been such good allies for so many centuries. We complement each other's strengths and weaknesses. Now will you come?"

"I will come."

"Good." He glanced at the sleeping children. "Can you leave them alone here for a while?"

"Yes."

"Then—"

"Kelly," she said with an odd urgency in her voice, "there is more. Segatha is not the enemy here."

Kelly's brows went up. He waited, aware that he wasn't going to like what he heard.

"There is Dausal. Dausal, my brother." She waited, but when he said nothing, she struggled on. "He betrayed my father to the DUR when we were trying to defect. He would not come with us. He broke my father's heart. Now they have given him this task of bringing me back. He is filled with hate. He will not let us get away."

"We'll persuade him otherwise."

"Kelly!" She reached out as though to grip his hand, but Kelly involuntarily drew back.

They stared at each other, their eyes locked, and in that instant Kelly's heart thundered with embarrassment.

"You have known blood-call," she whispered.

He wanted to go on meeting her eyes, but his own emotions and memories drove him to avert his gaze. "I have encountered it," he said grimly. "I don't want to do so again."

"It was not my intention," she said softly.

But her voice was like music, and he remembered 41's warning.

"Then let's keep it—"

"It is 41 I want," she said, still in that same soft voice.

Startled by that admission, Kelly stared at her openly then. "Aren't half-breeds taboo?"

"I have broken taboos before," she said, and he supposed she was referring to killing Pharaon Nefir.

"And if 41 denies you? Can you control blood-call?"

Some of the seriousness lightened in her face. "If it could be controlled, it would not be blood-call. But I am a long way from the vein-burn."

"I asked, what if 41 denies you?"

"Denies me?" she said, sounding almost amused. "No, Kelly. It is he who will hunt me. But not tonight," she went on as Kelly stood there, wondering what he could do to prevent it and even if he should try. "When he is well."

"Melaethia—"

She held up her hand imperiously. "You want me to hear the plans. You will give me a task to do. If I help you, Kelly, then you must not stand in my way."

There it was, a threat as gently implied as a sword beneath a veil. Kelly frowned at her, aware of the Salukan inclination for intrigue, wondering for the first time if she could be trusted at all.

"I don't want my friend hurt."

"You call a Salukan friend?"

"41 calls himself human. I respect that," said Kelly shortly. "You killed the last male you slept with, remember?"

Fury filled her face. Her eyes flashed at him, and her fingers curled to show her tiny claws. "You mock what you do not understand."

"I understand the dangers," he said. "Again, I don't want him hurt."

"And is he not a man, to decide for himself?"

Kelly's head went up. He realized, with a flush of shame, that he was interfering in 41's private life. "He can decide," Kelly said, but reluctance and worry made his voice rough.

She smiled, and the look of calculation in her eyes worried him more. "Then stand aside from the chase, if you do not wish to participate."

He didn't appreciate the warning. Cheeks hot, he said, "Just remember whose side you're on, Melaethia."

"Dausal," she said harshly, "will not let me forget."

8

The best strategy is that of surprise.

—maxim of Mailord General Viir

Ouoji crept belly-flat along the power feed conduit line. The top of the duct brushed her back, leaving traces of chemical dust on her fur. A growl kept rising in her throat. She hated this place. It was not good to be here.

But it was the only way to avoid the intruders.

She paused at a junction and crouched there, her senses attuned, her tail tip jerking angrily. Everyone belonging to her pride was still safe. She detected each in turn, picking up their anger and fears. Ouoji's tail lashed harder. She growled, empathizing strongly.

Then with a jerk of her head, she broke the connection. They wanted to make the ship theirs again. She would help.

She went on, burrowing her way farther along the conduit, until she reached the battery room itself. She waited a long while, her senses alert, for any of the stinking things to come into this area. None did. There were only two of the stinking things still alive. They did the bidding of the intruders.

Satisfied, she edged herself from her hiding place and crawled up beneath the lowest curve of the light scoop. The conversion generators supporting it hummed sleekly. She examined them a long while, aware that there was a way to open them, aware also that it was beyond her abilities. She must find something else.

The massive batteries lay on their mounts, brimming with stored power. A main power feed led off from them. She sat on her haunches and growled. To break power was dangerous. She did not want to destroy the ship or bring injury to any in her pride. When she got too close to the power feed, the fur rose along her spine, and she was afraid.

She found a systems check panel high above her head. Too high to reach, and without her little harness which could carry tools she did not think she could affect it.

Again she prowled about, worried and upset. She could smell Caesar's scent in here. His hands had touched many things. Siggerson had been here also. The scents were stronger between the batteries, along a tiny power line connecting them. Her ear flaps opened slightly in surprise. This was not as frightening. Their hands had been here.

She sniffed and peered beneath one of the batteries. Something lay beneath it. Ouoji fished with her paw until she managed to bring it out. The tubing, miniature tanks, and coils meant nothing to her. She had not seen such a thing before. But attached to one of the little tanks with a magnetic clamp was a laser probe.

She chittered softly in delight. She knew how to use a probe. Pawing quickly, she knocked it free of its clamp and bounded after it as it went rolling across the deck. Picking it up in her mouth, she brought it back to that tiny connecting line between the batteries.

Using tools was a slow business. She had to be very careful. Lining the probe up precisely on the deck so that its end pointed at the cable, she put one paw on the handle to secure it and carefully touched the ON button. A red light came to life, and she drew back from the faint hum at the probe's tip.

Then it was a matter of picking up the probe between her front paws, balancing herself upright on her haunches, and holding the tip steadily against the cable.

The steady hum from the conversion generator hiccuped. A red light began flashing on the systems check. Ouoji dropped the probe and watched in great satisfaction on her haunches, only to drop to all four paws seconds later when the system made some kind of adjustment and the red lights stopped flashing.

Her tail lashed back and forth, very hard. She must find something else to sabotage.

For a few moments she paced about, crying softly to herself, but the answer had always been before her. The batteries did not matter as long as the main engines were running. She could not get to the engines as long as the stinking thing guarded them.

She cried again, and her heart thumped in fear. But the fat power line lay pulsing before her, with all its tremendous energy barely contained within the cable housing.

For a while she considered going to Siggerson. Kelly would have made a plan by now, and Siggerson would give her orders and detailed instructions for what she should do.

But Ouoji knew that right now Kelly had no plan. Kelly's mind was dark with worry. Kelly had already once tried to initiate the destruct sequence, which must not be allowed. That showed Ouoji that he was not clear, that he was using his mind instead of his heart.

No, she could not depend on them. She must do this thing herself.

Her lips drew back and she hissed at the power line, but then she picked up the laser probe and carried it over. Again she lifted it between her paws, but this time she dropped it and had to jump nimbly to avoid the dangerous tip as it rolled past her. She recovered it and tried again. This time she succeeded in holding the tip to the cable.

It took longer, for the cable housing was thick. Tremors ran through her. Her own mind felt black with fear. She wanted to drop the probe and run away to a safe place of hiding, but she stayed put, holding the probe until her body ached from the unnatural position.

The cable was too tough. The probe was not getting through. She had better go down to deck three and try once more to slip into the engine room.

Defeated, she let the probe sag. At that very moment, she felt the tip puncture the resistance. Lights flashed all over the

systems panel. The feed line split, and as Ouoji jumped back
from it, howling in fear, energy spilled forth in a raw, sizzling
backlash of destruction.

Scrambling for a hiding place, Ouoji tried to scoot beneath
the conversion generators, but something exploded. She was
struck hard, so hard her entire body went numb and cold. There
was a sound that did not belong in this world, a shrill roaring
that deafened her although she clamped her ear flaps very tight.
Then she was struck again, and darkness ate her, and she was
glad.

Down in the mess lounge, the stew was hot and tasty.
Wrapped in thought, Kelly ate steadily, aware that his body
needed nourishment and rest. There wasn't much talk. Everyone looked tired.

Melaethia sat wedged firmly between Phila and Beaulieu.
She did not eat much and she did not speak at all. Caesar, one
eyebrow charred and his face shiny from burn ointment, was
scowling and eating fast as though anxious to get on with his
job. Phila looked preoccupied. Siggerson was simply in a bad
mood. Beaulieu had on her analytical look, which meant she
was measuring each of them for stress. 41 stayed in his corner
on the floor, eating, but looking far too pale.

"There's seven of us, and five of them," said Phila. "Those
odds aren't bad."

"They've got all the weapons, toots," said Caesar, and took
a third helping of stew. "And where's seven? Count out Mel,
41, and Siggie-boy, and that leaves four. We're the underdogs,
and the odds *are* bad."

"Why should I be counted out?" demanded Siggerson. "Just
because the normal course of my duties does not pitch me into
combat as frequently as—"

"Oh, get stuffed," said Caesar, rolling his eyes.

Siggerson's spoon rattled inside his bowl. "I have gone
through all the munitions drills. My score on the testing range
was sufficient to—"

"Scores don't mean squat."

"Can it, both of you," said Kelly. "You've shown in the past
that the two of you can work together when you want. I think

it's time you stopped squabbling like adolescents and put some—"

41 threw his bowl across the room, and the resulting crash and splat of stew upon the wall made them all look at him in startlement.

Kelly rose from his chair. "41, what the devil—"

But 41 wasn't listening, didn't even appear to hear Kelly. He was staring wide-eyed into space, then he flung off his blanket and tried to get to his feet.

"Ouoji!" he yelled. "*No!*"

"What is it?" said Kelly, starting toward him. "What's—"

He never finished his query, for just then space bent around him. One second the room looked perfectly ordinary; the next, it seemed to be folded at right angles to itself. Hearing cries of consternation from the others, Kelly held out his arms in astonishment. His arms were bending the wrong way. He seemed to see himself from the side, which was not possible, unless . . .

"Distort hole!" he yelled, only it came out all wrong, more like, "DDDDDistttttooooorrrtt hoooollllleeee!"

He tried to turn, tried to run for the bridge, but every movement went the wrong way. The room bent further; now it was curving. The distortion effect spread rapidly, blurring outlines and making multiple doors. The color spectrum appeared around their faces. He could hear them calling out, but he could not understand the words.

Increasing pressure meant the stabilizers were unable to cope with mounting g forces. Prickles danced over his skin as though an electrical charge was building too. He saw Phila's and Melaethia's hair standing on end.

Something had to be done and fast. Kelly had been in plenty of simulations to train him how to cope with distort problems, but there was something peculiar about this. They didn't have the jarring vibrations that came from falling into a spatial anomaly.

"DDDDooooowwwwnnnnn!" yelled Siggerson. He passed Kelly in a blur of wrong shapes. "SSSllaaaammm ccoooom-mmiiiiinnggggg soooooonn!"

Slam coming soon. Comprehension flashed into Kelly's

mind. They hadn't hit an anomaly or fallen into a hole. They had engine problems. Serious ones.

He threw himself to the deck although the fall seemed to take forever. Watching his outstretched hands, Kelly thought he'd hit long before he felt the actual thud of impact. He managed to grab hold of something solid and cling to it.

And then slam came as they plummetted from time distortion speed into the reality of their normal dimension. The ship rolled and shuddered. Gritting his teeth against the excruciating pressure on his eyeballs and inner ears, Kelly heard the tortured squawl of the *Sabre* as though she was being torn inside out.

He wanted to scream with her. He thought he was being crushed to death, and he told himself to hang on, just hang on.

Then miraculously the terrible pressure ended. Kelly opened his eyes to find the lounge back to its usual shape and size. The lights, however, were flickering erratically. The air had a curious ozone smell. The ship was vibrating now, with lurches and squawling shudders that told him she was out of control.

Kelly pushed himself to his feet, staggering across the canted deck, and knelt beside Siggerson, who was still making aimless groggy movements.

Kelly gripped his shoulder. "Come on, man! Pull yourself together. We've got to reach the bridge."

Siggerson's head came up sharply. "She's out of control. She'll pull herself apart. Something with the—"

"Never mind. Just come on!"

Kelly hauled him to his feet. As they passed the others, Kelly met Caesar's eyes.

"This is our chance," he said. "Make whatever move you can. Go for the Jostics first. The Salukans are less dangerous."

"Right, boss." Caesar turned to give Beaulieu and Phila a hand up. Melaethia was already running for the door to check on her children.

"Oh, and Caesar?"

"Yo?"

Kelly gave him a thumbs up for luck. "Don't get yourself killed."

"You neither," said Caesar, and grinned.

* * *

Kelly hoped that the Jostic guard posted on the ladder well had been knocked unconscious by slam, but no such luck. In fact, the guard was coming down the corridor toward them, blaster in hand, making urgent, snuffling grunts.

When he saw Kelly and Siggerson, he gestured. Siggerson quickened his speed to a run. Kelly eyed the blaster and decided not to try anything right now. He followed Siggerson, but the Jostic's forearm whacked across Kelly's chest, nearly knocking the wind from him.

"I need to be up there too," said Kelly.

The Jostic's orange eyes gleamed piggishly. His tongue darted over his crooked, half-rotted teeth. He pushed Kelly into the wall. Kelly stepped away from it to avoid being pinned there.

"One man can't handle whatever's wrong," said Kelly. "We need to—"

"Trick," said the Jostic. "Minlord believe you. I not. No, I not. Know trick. Break power feed. Ship go spinning. Big trick. Work good. But I know trick."

He shoved Kelly. Kelly was thinking fast, backing up a step or two at a time, leading the Jostic down the corridor closer to the lounge where Caesar and Phila waited. Jostics were almost impossible to fight hand-to-hand. They were built short and squat, for one thing, and set upon bowed, sturdy legs. That meant their center of gravity was low, and it was difficult to shift them off-balance. Their skeletons were hard-density bone, about twice as strong as human bone. Their joints were rubbery interlocks of cartilage and fiber. Their skin was as tough as leather. Vulnerable spots were hard to find.

The Jostic swung without warning. Just in time Kelly managed to duck inside the blow, which glanced harmlessly off his shoulder. He heard the Jostic howl in rage, but Kelly had already gripped his wrist and slammed his weight against the Jostic to shift him into the wall in an effort to make him drop the blaster.

The Jostic's free fist clutched Kelly's tunic and twisted it, pulling Kelly off and slinging him across the corridor. Kelly hit the far wall and turned, his heart in his throat as he expected to die. But before the Jostic could shoot, Caesar had pounced on him, and Phila too.

Howling, the Jostic struggled to throw them off, but Phila jammed a fork into his mouth. The yells ceased abruptly. The Jostic's face turned a queer color. His eyes flickered and went dead. He toppled over like a stone.

"You okay, boss?" said Caesar, panting.

Kelly nodded and pushed himself away from the wall. Phila crouched over the Jostic and plucked away his blaster, the agonizer device on his belt, and his torch. Only after she had kicked him a couple of times did she remove the fork and clean it on the Jostic's sleeve.

"Yusus," said Caesar in disgust. "You're getting as savage as 41. You going to take scalps too?"

Phila's face was absolutely expressionless. There was no regret and no doubt in her black eyes as she lifted them scornfully to Caesar. She came upright and faced him. "It's the only way to kill *cosquenti* like that quick and quiet. The central brain cortex is right behind the back of the throat. One good thrust through the thin cartilage there, and—"

"We get the idea," said Kelly hastily, frowning.

She tossed back her hair and scowled at both of them. "Don't look at me like that! They made raids on my home-world often before the defense satellites were put up. We learned what to do. Give a Jostic mercy and he'll kill you. Ever had one of your relatives eaten, Caesar?"

"All right. All right," said Caesar. "Geesh, don't get all riled about it. I just asked."

"You can't afford to get squeamish with a Jostic," she said without relenting. "I learned that the hard way."

Caesar frowned at her, then turned to Kelly, who said, "Clear him from the corridor. Phila, give Caesar the weapons and get up to the bridge to help Siggerson. I'll—"

"41!" yelled Beaulieu from inside the lounge. "Dammit, don't you—"

"Kelly," said 41 breathlessly, appearing in the doorway. He sagged against the wall, his color its color, and looked at Kelly. "Ouoji needs help."

Kelly remembered that 41 had sensed something wrong with

their mascot just before all hell broke loose. Instead of telling
41 that he needed to be in bed, which was useless advice, Kelly
said, "You sensed she was in trouble. What—"

"I think she made this happen. We must not waste the
chance we have now, but she needs help."

Beaulieu appeared beside him, glaring. "I don't want this
man on his feet, Commander."

"Doctor—"

"No! 41 may have a pronounced macho complex, but I take
you for a man with better sense. If he walks on that leg, he's
going to reopen the wound. With sickbay closed off, I don't
have access to transfusions. You've leaked enough of that
damned yellow stuff you call blood, 41. If you lose any
more—"

41 turned from her and limped into the corridor. Kelly met
Beaulieu's furious gaze and just shook his head.

"Hey!" said Caesar. "You can't use that ladder. The hatch's
been welded shut. Go the main way."

41 came back, his face knotted with effort, limping heavily.
As he drew even with them once again, Phila held out the fork.
He took it with an approving glimmer in his eyes.

"Go on, Phila," said Kelly quietly.

She nodded and hurried for the bridge.

Caesar picked up one of the Jostic's feet and heaved.
"Weighs a metric ton," he muttered.

Kelly smiled at 41 to hide his concern. "We'll go together."

Behind them, Kelly heard Caesar say impatiently, "Don't
just stand there having a tizzy, Doc. Lend a hand."

Not until Kelly and 41 were out of sight inside the ladder
well, did 41 sag against the wall and pass a hand across his
face.

"Hurting?"

41 nodded. He slid the fork out of sight up his sleeve and
eyed the ladder wearily. "It must be done."

"If you'd asked, she would have given you a painkiller,"
said Kelly.

41 snorted. "Beaulieu thinks she is a god instead of a
female."

"Doctors tend to get that way."

"It is enough to let her tend me," said 41. "I try to follow the human ways, but I tell you, Kelly, she gives too many orders in what concerns her not."

"If you'd stop getting yourself shot full of holes," said Kelly mildly, "you wouldn't have to listen to her as often."

41 considered this a moment, then bared his teeth. "True," he said less angrily. "Do you go first?"

"No, you'd better. Do you think you can make it all the way up?" asked Kelly.

41 didn't answer. He went up the ladder fairly quickly, using two hands and one leg, his wounded one dangling. Kelly could hear his harsh breathing, and worried but said nothing. When 41 made up his mind to do something, there was no deflecting him.

They stepped onto the bridge cautiously, and then Kelly forgot everything else as he stared at the chaos. The viewscreen should have been switched off, for the dizzying blur of constellations told Kelly at once that they were spinning completely out of control. If the internal stabilizers had not continued to hold, they would all have been tumbled to death by now.

Siggerson was working feverishly at the master station, snapping orders to Phila and the Salukan Chuteph alike. Segatha stood to one side, his lean elegant figure braced against the heavy vibrations in the ship, his face grave. Pacing back and forth was the third Salukan, Melaethia's infamous brother Dausal.

Either Dausal did not at all resemble his father and sister, or sons of traitors were tortured very harshly indeed. Kelly's gaze narrowed at the bowed, crooked shoulders, and the shortened leg that made Dausal hobble in a lurching gait. His face was scarred and stained blue in irregular patches.

Tyrsian salt, thought Kelly. This man had been in the mines. The fact that he'd survived said a lot for his toughness. But when he glanced Kelly's way, his eyes looked half-mad.

"You did this!" he said hoarsely. "Get out. You'll work no more sabotage on this ship."

Segatha stepped toward Kelly. His gaze, however, went to 41. "We did not revive everyone from the gas to allow you free run—"

"Look," said Kelly impatiently. "Right now we're in plenty of trouble. We know how to operate this ship. You don't. Keeping us locked up doesn't mean squat right now."

"Can you help?"

"Minlord!" said Dausal. "Kelly is not to be on the bridge. I have given that order. I want it carried out. And that—that abomination—"

41 turned on him with bared teeth. "You intend to be Vaudan, the Right Hand of Pharaon?" he said scornfully in Saluk. "Then know that I have dominated your Pharaon, and when there is training to be done he will look to me for it."

The effort of this announcement upon the Salukans was immediate. Segatha stiffened, Chuteph threw down his tools in visible horror, and Dausal came limping across the bridge.

"Lies!" he shouted. "Creature spawned of filth and degradation, you will not speak so proudly when you are under the mind sieve."

"There won't be any mind sieves," said Kelly sharply. "We aren't going to make it to Gamael like this. In fact we'll be lucky if we don't hit an asteroid or planetary body. You'd better worry less about your political ambitions and more about the fate of this ship right now. Mr. Siggerson, what's our status?"

Siggerson was working inside the circuit panel and never looked up, but his voice was crisp as he replied, "*Sabre* is out of control. Navigation and helm are blown. Main power transformer is not firing. Generators are off line. Batteries have been disconnected from systems supports. Cannot determine whether reserve power is intact at this time. We have major power leakage in the light scoop area. Radiation contamination levels are rising one-half percent every half hour."

"Can you stop us from this crazy spin?" asked Kelly, his mouth very dry.

Siggerson touched something very delicately and sparks flew. "I'm attempting to reach braking thrusters now. If I can get a manual override wired in—"

He bent over, concentrating on his task and did not complete his sentence. Kelly met 41's eyes. *Ouoji*, said 41's lips in silence. Kelly nodded, feeling sick about it. He knew Ouoji had to be where the leakage was, where the radiation contamination was.

With a fast decision, he turned to Segatha and said, "The leak has to be stopped. If 41 and I go in there wearing environmental suits, I think we have a chance of containing it. But if we let radiation levels get too high, then the emergency bridge seal won't protect this area, or the rest of the ship."

"Do it," said Segatha.

"Minlord—" began Dausal in protest, but Segatha turned on him fiercely.

"Would you rather risk your life or theirs? It must be done. Let them work before Shevul takes all of us."

Opening lockers in the back of the bridge, Kelly and 41 donned environmental suits, checking seals and air feeds with quick efficiency. Clamping on the faceplate, Kelly tapped his comm line, and 41 answered.

It was necessary to override the bridge seal on the corridor leading to the battery room. Kelly had a meter which tracked the radiation levels. It was getting close to the point where neither the seal nor the suits would be any protection.

Phila brought them a tool kit. "Safe flight," she whispered.

Kelly read her lips through his faceplate and motioned her to step back. They went through quickly, and resealed the door before opening the inner seal. Kelly switched his comm to open receiving and was able to pick up the sounds coming from the battery room.

It was an eerie ululation such as he had never heard before. Clutching the tool kit tighter than he needed to, he crept down the short corridor and peered into the battery room.

The place was lit with spangled, yellow energy pouring through the broken power feed and filling the room with its deadly beauty. Kelly's heart sank. He did not think they could contain such damage. But 41 was moving forward, limping awkwardly around the narrow space between the generators and the wall. The light scoop was still functioning, causing part of the problem.

Kelly opened a line to Siggerson.

"Siggerson here. How bad is it?"

"Bad," said Kelly. "Split in the main power feed. Can you shut off power?"

"To the engines?" said Siggerson. "They aren't in operation. We're going on sheer momentum. Considering our velocity at the time of slam, I still don't know how we survived without cracking up."

"Can you shut off the light scoop?"

"Affirmative. But I don't think—"

"Siggerson," said Kelly impatiently, "it's still pouring juice in here. We can't do repairs with—"

"Understood," said Siggerson. "Are the batteries still holding reserves? If they're out and I shut off the light scoop we'll really be dead. In every sense of the word."

"Checking now," said Kelly.

Gingerly, wary of stepping directly into the energy stream, Kelly ran a quick systems check on the batteries. "Siggerson, one is full. The other is three-quarters drained. Something broke their connecting line."

"A miracle," said Siggerson. "All right. Shutting down light scoop now. Stand by to manually switch on the battery reserve."

"Standing by."

Seconds went by—long seconds. Kelly stood there and watched the radiation meter climb. 41 was still searching, slowly and methodically. By now Kelly almost wanted to tell him to stop. Ouoji, if here, must surely be dead.

The base panel of the light scoop was about eye level for Kelly. It flashed an intricate series of red and green lights. Then everything went red and stayed there. With a sizzling hiss, the noise of the energy wave stopped, and the golden stream of light faded into gloom.

Kelly tripped a switch and neutralizing radiation sprayed from the walls and ceiling. That stuff wasn't exactly a prime environment for people either, but it was the only way to clean this up. Kelly walked over to the power cable, which was as thick as his upper arm. Rummaging in the tool kit, he picked out the clamps and a delicate laser welder. He checked the wall lockers for spare parts and found a huge repair coupler that would fit. He clamped it in place, sweating despite the falling temperature, and welded it a lot less neatly than he would have preferred. His hands weren't steady enough. He didn't know if it was from nerves or fatigue. The idea of botching this and having another split occur made him sweat harder.

He put away the welder at last, but left the clamps on. "Siggerson," he said.

Siggerson's voice came back promptly.

"I've got a repair coupler in place," said Kelly. "What's next? Will it hold?"

"It should. But not for anything above mere impulse. That cable is made of a semi-organic fiber woven with chemical molecules that actually bond more strongly the more power is fed through. The couplers aren't of the same material, and they can't be more than temporary."

"I've done all I can here," said Kelly. "I'm going into decon, then we'd better discuss what—"

"Kelly," said Segatha's voice over the comm, "I'm missing one of the Jostic guards. What have you—"

"The hell with your guards!" said Kelly, losing his temper in a sudden burst. "My God, man, we're talking basic survival here. You—"

"I think you have been sabotaging your own ship. I think this was planned and one of your team executed this disaster. You will return now."

Kelly glared a moment at the far wall, trying to rein in his anger. "I'll return," he said shortly, "as soon as I've been through decontamination. Unless you'd like a good dose of radiation sickness to go along with your other troubles. You can monitor us inside the chamber if you're suspicious of tricks."

Segatha did not reply. Kelly broke the connection and stood up with a sigh. When he turned around, he came up short at the sight of 41 standing there in the bulky white environmental suit, holding a tattered length of fur in his hands.

Ouoji's stillness, the limp drape of her legs and tail over 41's wrist, and 41's own silence made Kelly's heart squeeze with grief. He stared at them a long, long moment until he managed to force himself to ask the question.

"Dead?"

"I do not know," said 41. "I do not sense her. In this suit I cannot feel her heart. There is not much chance."

His voice was stone cold, giving away nothing, yet giving away everything.

Kelly bowed his head, feeling hot tears rush into his eyes. He blinked them back. "She did this for us, didn't she?"

41 turned away, carrying her gently. "Let us take her from this place."

9

O Ru, God of Light . . . how fierce art thine eyes . . . how dread is thy visage. Take mercy upon thy people. Rise over them gently. Return from the night.

—ancient prayer

Segatha's laughter, half-amused, half-incredulous, filled the air. "You wish me to unlock the dispensary for an *animal*?"

"Ouoji is a sentient Minzanese life form," said Kelly, trying to keep anger and frustration from his voice. "She's more than an animal."

"You mock me with this game," said Segatha. His earlier poise had vanished. Now he paced nervously, restlessly about the bridge, holding a blaster in his hand. Chuteph stood impassively to one side. Dausal had vanished. "Throw the creature in the disposal chute and get on with your work."

"No!" said Siggerson, taking a half-step forward. "You heartless bastard, if there's any chance to save her we've got to try—"

A bolt from Segatha's blaster singed past Siggerson's sleeve and burned a hole in a station chair. Siggerson flinched back, cursing. Kelly steadied him and glanced at 41, who was still holding Ouoji, his face taut with hostility.

"That was stupid," said Kelly in a low, harsh voice. "Siggerson's the only skilled pilot available."

"Yes, and what good is he if he will not work?" retorted
Segatha. "Would you rather I shot this half-breed?"

Not by as much as a flicker did Kelly betray his concern for
41. He held Segatha's contemptuous gaze steadily. "Let us
open the sickbay and put Ouoji in a life-support capsule."

"No."

"You—"

The blaster again swung Siggerson's way. Kelly put a quick
hand on Siggerson's hand to shut him up. The pilot's face was
beet red and contorted with grief. He stood there, clenching
and unclenching his fists. His eyes met Kelly's in a mute
appeal to do something.

"Is this," said Kelly, "just another example of Salukan
inability to show mercy, or do you have some reason for your
cruelty?"

"I am not a fool," said Segatha. "I know you have sabotaged
this ship. Now you want access to your medical laboratory and
chemicals in order to—"

"No," said Kelly. "Let 41 enter the sickbay. Guard him and
watch everything he does. Let him put Ouoji in the capsule,
activate it, and walk out. That's all we ask."

"And I am expected to agree to this? Agree tamely?"

"Do it!" said Siggerson desperately, unable to keep quiet
any longer. "I'll get us back on course somehow. I know how
to cross-connect the—"

"Agreed," said Segatha. His eyes were slits, however, of
suspicion. He pointed at the master station. "Work. Now. If
you fail, pilot, I shall kill the creature before your very eyes."

The color drained from Siggerson's face. He gave a jerky
nod of agreement, touched Ouoji's head briefly, and went back
to work.

Segatha gestured at Chuteph, who walked toward 41.
Together they left the bridge.

Kelly joined Siggerson at the master station. Siggerson's
shoulders were hunched, and he was breathing audibly. His
hands trembled.

Kelly squeezed his forearm. "Steady," he said in a low
voice.

"She'll die," whispered Siggerson. "She'll die. Too much radiation—"

"Stop it," said Kelly sharply. "Ouoji didn't commit that act of heroism just so you could botch things now."

His harshness was calculated, and it worked. Siggerson lifted his head. His eyes had the flat sheen of tears. He wiped his face. "No," he said raggedly. "No, I guess not. I—"

"Pull yourself together. Start thinking. Are we still spinning?"

Siggerson nodded. He kept his gaze down, not looking at Kelly.

"Any control?" said Kelly. "What about those braking thrusters?"

"Waiting until you came out of there," said Siggerson. He cleared his throat. "Uh, we have some percentage of the gyro computer back on line. I can re-engage power just enough to fire the braking thrusters without blowing out your repair. I—I haven't plotted our new trajectory yet. We'd better have plenty of room."

Satisfied that Siggerson was beginning to function again, Kelly switched on the astrogation panel and called up a star chart. He located their position and graphed out their course heading. It was erratic, but fortunately they were traveling along a fairly empty vector of space.

"Approaching no star systems or asteroid belts," he said in relief. "We're close to this system, however. If you kick us in that direction?"

Siggerson frowned. "Why? With our weak pulse power we could be caught into a gravitational orbit. We'd—"

"Exactly," said Kelly. He looked at Siggerson and saw the dawning comprehension in the pilot's eyes. At once Kelly pivoted and moved around the master station with a glance toward Segatha, who was watching, still slit-eyed with suspicion.

Segatha came over. "What are you plotting?"

Kelly's forefinger traced their heading. "Just checking to make sure we have maneuvering room," he said. "We'll be firing the braking thrusters to bring us back under control. I'd hate to run into something by mistake."

"We are very close to that system," said Segatha, pointing.

Kelly's gut tightened. But he'd played poker long enough to keep his feelings off his face when he needed to. He nodded.

"You will want to spin the ship away from that sun," said Segatha. "Graph the course heading for Gamael. Make an overlay."

Kelly complied and Segatha nodded. "There," he said, stabbing his finger down. "Calculate the turn needed to put us back on course. How long?"

Kelly glanced at Siggerson, who said with some of his old irritableness, "Don't rush me. These calculations are complex and without the astrogation computer linked up properly with helm right now, I must not make a mistake. I'll tell you when it's time."

"Very well," said Segatha, "but remember that as long as we are using battery reserve power for life support, your dispensary unit has lowest priority and will be shut off when necessary."

Siggerson's head snapped up at the threat. Segatha looked at him without blinking, making sure Siggerson knew the exact penalty for trickery.

"You don't want your pet to die, do you?" said Segatha softly.

And Siggerson dropped his gaze first.

Kelly could have throttled Segatha, but before he could finish mastering his own exasperation, there came the clanging echo of someone running up the ladder. Chuteph burst onto the bridge, blaster drawn, and a wildness in his eyes that told Kelly there was fresh trouble.

Thinking it had to do with 41, Kelly stepped forward, but Chuteph aimed his blaster at Kelly. "Kuprat-eater! You will not get away with—"

"*Aret chese!*" snapped Segatha, and Chuteph whirled away from Kelly and pulled himself to stiff attention. "What is this behavior? Where is your prisoner?"

Chuteph's eyes slid around to glare at Kelly. He said, "Minlord, they have killed the Jostics—"

"*Quesa?*"

"Truly," said Chuteph as Segatha stared at him in shock.

"When I found the one assigned to deck two lying dead and hidden, I checked with my scanner. No Jostic life signs on deck three. The Earthers have—"

"May Than smite you!" shouted Segatha. He raised his own blaster and fired at Kelly, who ducked just in time.

The bolt of energy scored the edge of the viewscreen. Kelly squirmed for inadequate cover behind a chair, and a second bolt sizzled just centimeters above his head. Kelly heard Siggerson shout something, but he couldn't make it out.

Then the braking thrusters fired, and the *Sabre* bucked with a violence that sent Kelly slamming into the wall. For a moment he couldn't breathe, and he wondered if his ribs were still intact. Gathering himself, he stole a quick look, saw Chuteph down and Segatha on his hands and knees.

Kelly tackled Segatha from behind, driving him to the floor with bruising force. Segatha grunted and squirmed fiercely in an effort to throw Kelly off. Straddling Segatha's back, Kelly hooked his left arm around Segatha's throat, aware that the tough cartilage there wasn't going to let him do much damage that way, and punched Segatha in the upper torso where Salukans were vulnerable. He heard Segatha grunt in pain, then Segatha's elbow crashed into Kelly's stomach, driving all the air from his lungs.

Kelly's muscles went to water. Hot, aching nausea rose within him, and his hold slackened as he tried not to be sick. In that one vulnerable moment Segatha whipped onto his side, grabbed Kelly by the throat, and pulled him down in a swift roll that left Segatha on top.

Segatha's fingers were steel clamps, tightening steadily. Kelly tugged frantically at those fingers, but he could not loosen them. His air was going. Little dots danced before his eyes, blurring the sight of Segatha crouched over him.

Kelly punched hard, catching Segatha in the face. The awful pressure on his throat eased off momentarily, and Kelly drew up one knee swiftly to deliver a dirty kick. Segatha toppled back, cursing him in Saluk. Kelly dragged in a leaden breath and threw himself across Segatha, reaching for the minlord's House dagger.

Segatha twisted, and Kelly's fingers just skimmed the hilt.

Segatha drew the dagger and struck. Kelly seized his wrist with both hands and managed to deflect the sharp point away from his own shoulder. With cunning, Segatha suddenly stopped pushing and pulled in an effort to yank Kelly off-balance.

But Kelly knew better than to let himself be caught by that old trick. He threw himself at Segatha, going at the minlord faster than Segatha had obviously expected. Kelly saw a split-second glimmer of dismay in the Salukan's eyes before he executed a one-handed series of vicious chops directed at vital nerve centers.

Segatha's eyes rolled back in his head. He fell backward without a sound.

Panting hard, Kelly snatched the dagger from Segatha's slack fingers and whirled on Chuteph. But Chuteph still wasn't moving. Kelly looked around quickly and picked up Segatha's blaster from beneath a chair. Then he went cautiously to Chuteph and nudged the Salukan with his toe. Kelly disarmed him cautiously, wary of tricks, until he saw the blood beneath Chuteph's head and knew he was genuinely unconscious.

Straightening, Kelly checked out his aching ribs with careful fingers. Not broken, but they sure hurt. He went to the master station and put one of the blasters on the console where Siggerson could reach it.

"Good timing, Olaf," he said, wiping his mouth and trying to slow his breathing. "You hit those thrusters just in—"

"I did *not*," said Siggerson with such violence Kelly gave him a second look. The pilot was sweating profusely. His gaze was locked on his instrumentation. Lights were flashing.

Kelly instantly knew something was wrong—badly wrong. "What's the problem?" he said at once.

"Everything! I missed the calculation somehow. Or I fired the thrusters too late, too soon, who knows? Our velocity's so erratic I can't predict . . . and the power level is jumping dangerously."

"Siggerson," said Kelly, "we'll handle it. Remain calm. Tell me what to do."

Siggerson flashed him one, frantic glance. "Don't you understand? I missed the target. We're heading right into that system."

"All right," said Kelly, feeling Siggerson's fear catch at him and fighting it down. It was imperative he keep his head, or Siggerson would lose his for sure. "We missed the planet we wanted. We'll be caught in another orbit."

"That's not it! Look, dammit. Look!" Siggerson's hands fumbled over the controls and the viewscreen came on. "We're going into the sun. Another sixty-five seconds and we won't be able to break its gravitational pull."

Kelly stared at the fiery orb filling the screen. A blank whiteness washed through his mind, and he froze for an instant only. Then he forced himself to look away, refusing to be mesmerized by the danger.

"Stand by to fire braking thrusters again," he said. "Run those calculations fast, mister."

"Impossible," whispered Siggerson. He'd stopped working and was staring now at the viewscreen as though all hope had left him.

Fury overwhelmed Kelly. He gripped Siggerson by the arms, whipping him around, and shook him hard.

"Siggerson!" he shouted, "make those calculations! Now! If I have to hold that repair coupler in place with my hands I'll do it, but get ready to fire those thrusters again."

"Can't," said Siggerson, making no effort to extricate himself from Kelly's punishing grip. "When we fired the first time, the generators skewed from the strain. They're out. We can't convert sufficiently to raise enough power. The reserves don't have enough either. It's hopeless."

Kelly released him and stepped back, staring hard into the man's eyes. There had to be some flicker of gumption left in Siggerson.

"I refuse to believe in hopeless," said Kelly. "There must be something you can do—"

"No, there's nothing!" shouted Siggerson. "Don't you think I'd try if I could? She's got nothing left to give us. We've killed her."

Kelly heard the raw quiver in Siggerson's voice. He brushed past the pilot and reached for the in-ship comm. "Kelly calling," he said. "Kelly to lower decks. Caesar? 41? Phila? I need all hands on the bridge."

Sweat dripped into his eyes. It was getting very warm on the bridge, as though life support was growing unable to compensate for increasing hull temperature. Kelly saw the sun looming ever larger on the viewscreen, and forced himself again not to look at it. Siggerson made dispirited stabs at a couple of controls.

"Better they don't watch it happen," he muttered.

Kelly ignored him and tapped impatiently on the comm. "Kelly to lower decks. Respond. We have emergency. Repeat, emergency on the bridge. All hands report to bridge."

"Forty-eight seconds," said Siggerson.

"What the *hell* is happening down there?" said Kelly in frustration and renewed alarm. "Why don't they answer? Siggerson, are the comm circuits out?"

Before Siggerson could answer, Caesar's voice came in through a background hubbub of shouting and frantic screaming.

"Caesar!" said Kelly. "What's—"

". . . sorry, boss. Couldn't stop him. Should have known better . . ."

The screaming was growing more hysterical. Kelly could barely hear Caesar. He didn't understand, but right now it hardly mattered.

"Caesar, I need you and 41 on the bridge. Can Phila get into the engine room?"

Without waiting for Caesar's reply, Kelly turned on Siggerson. "Are you *sure* we can't fire those thrusters again? Can we jettison anything? Salvage the emergency life pod thrusters?"

"Too long to convert," said Siggerson, staring at a data graph that was wavering visibly. "Forty-one seconds."

Kelly slapped him, and the whipcrack sound of flesh upon flesh echoed in the air. Kelly's palm stung, and he curled his fingers into a fist. "I don't want a countdown, mister," he said icily. "I want action. I refuse to give up and I refuse to let anyone around me give up. Now think of a solution!"

Siggerson stared at him, wide-eyed and silent with shock. Red marks from Kelly's fingers burned across his cheek. Otherwise, he had gone deathly pale. The moment seemed endless, but Kelly never let his furious gaze waver for an instant. If discipline wouldn't make Siggerson move, perhaps shame would.

Kelly shoved him aside with enough force to send Siggerson staggering completely away from the master station. Kelly began tapping controls rapidly, using adrenaline to carry him over unfamiliarity with some of the systems. He had a standard working knowledge of everything on this ship, of course, or he couldn't command her, but that was a long way from actually handling her on his own.

Right now, it didn't matter. He *was* on his own, and his mind was going lightning fast.

"Siggerson," he said, hating the man right now for his cowardice and inaction, "I want to jump. Start feeding the calculations into the helm directional as the astrogator calls them up."

"You're crazy," said Siggerson. "We haven't the power. We can't."

"We do and we will."

"That coupler will blow. I told you it can't hold, and besides, there's no conversion. The generators are out."

"We have battery reserves, don't we?" shouted Kelly.

From the corner of his eye, he saw Phila come running onto the bridge. He looked at her in relief.

"Phila, good. There's no link between astrogation and helm. You come here and enter these figures by hand—"

"Kelly," she said, panting. "There's trouble—"

"Lots of it," he said without paying any attention. He pushed her into place at the master station. "Siggerson, start priming the main thrusters."

"You're mad," said Siggerson. "You can't ever face defeat, can you? You refuse to see facts and their unpleasant realities. You always think you can pull off the impossible."

He was useless. He had made up his mind that they were finished, and some stupid quirk in his brain wanted to be proven right. Kelly frowned at him and veered away to prime the main thrusters himself. Thirty seconds . . . *don't think about the time*.

"And," said Siggerson, talking over the sound of Phila counting softly out loud as she concentrated on entering figures, "the relays to the engine room are out. It has to be a manual jump, and even you have to admit that we can't get that timing right."

Kelly gave him no acknowledgment, just opened the comm line again. "Kelly to Caesar. Kelly to 41. Someone, come in."

"Caesar here. Boss, we got a—"

"Listen," said Kelly sharply. "One of you get into the engine room now and keep the comm open."

"Boss—"

"No questions," said Kelly. "We've got very few seconds to spare. Locate the time distort panel. We've got to do a manual jump."

"*Criminy—*"

"Do it, dammit, or we're dead!" shouted Kelly.

"Yo," said Caesar, and broke the line.

Only then did Kelly become conscious that he was hunched over the comm, his hands gripping the edges of the console as though to force his will along that electronic signal. Sweat drenched him, and not all of it was caused by the heat.

"Hull sensors are overloading," said Siggerson from another station. "Hull temperature now—"

"Shut up," snapped Kelly. He glanced at Phila, who had turned absolutely white as she grasped the situation but stood resolute to do her duty. He gave her a brief smile, then faced the glowing digits on the chron. Was there enough time for Caesar to get into the engine room?

"Sir," whispered Phila. "The Salukan Dausal has barricaded himself on deck three. I'm not sure they can get through."

The news hit Kelly low, sapping his energy suddenly. But he hid his dismay and summoned optimism in its place. "We've done our best," he said. "Time for a leap of faith."

"Literally," growled Siggerson. "Splintered on a time curve, our hull shattered and our—"

"When we burn up, it won't matter," said Kelly angrily.

Warning lights flashed everywhere, even the one over the door that signaled life support failure. The heat had gone beyond stifling to unbearable. Even the air shimmered with it, making the bridge look as though it were under water. Surfaces became hot, both from the rising temperature and from internal overheating.

Phila swept her hands up her face and over the top of her hair, then bent over the graphs. "Nominals," she reported. "Pretty shaky. We've got a leak somewhere."

"I know," said Kelly, thinking of his repair that would blow under the strain. "Stand by."

"Four seconds," said Siggerson hoarsely.

Kelly touched the comm. "Caesar," he said urgently. "Now!"

Nothing happened.

"He couldn't get through," said Phila. "That stupid Salukan kept him from getting through!"

And on the bridge, the three of them faced the fiery sun that now filled the viewscreen in its entirety. Yellow-white, shooting off the great solar flares from its seething mass, it was dazzling, blinding . . . terrifying.

The polarization on the screen could no longer compensate. Abruptly the screen went black and empty.

"We're past the point of breakaway," said Siggerson into the grim, hot silence. "We're burning up."

10

Defeat is found in the mind, not in the arm.

—from the Warrior's Code

On deck two, Caesar had just spun away from the comm to obey Kelly's orders when Melaethia darted past Beaulieu and blocked access to the ladder.

"No," she said, her voice raw with hysteria. "You will not go down there. You will not endanger my son."

Caesar drew his weapon and held it ready, exchanging an exasperated glance with 41. "I'm not gonna argue with this babe. What's the Saluk word for move?"

"*Hut! Maitain*!" snapped 41.

Melaethia raised her chin. "You're fools. Dausal will kill him. It is no bluff."

41 limped toward her. "You are the fool," he said harshly. "The boy-child is too important to Dausal."

"You see the obvious only!" she screamed. "There is more to it than—"

41 seized her by the wrist and forced her aside. She twisted and called down the well, "Dausal! *Avi*—"

41 grabbed her around the middle and clapped his hand over her mouth. Her enraged squawl was muffled as she clawed at

121

him. Caesar slipped past them as they grappled, and hustled himself down the ladder as fast as he could.

Weariness sagged into his bones. He was getting very tired of assaulting deck three. Did this make three times, or four? He couldn't remember. It didn't matter because he had to do it again.

Above him he could still hear Melaethia screaming and cursing in Saluk like something gone demented. They had no chance of catching Dausal unawares now, if there had ever been a chance.

Seconds, Kelly had said, sounding hoarse—sounding *scared*. The ship must be in bad trouble, worse than anything they'd encountered yet. Worse even than that distort hole they'd fallen into.

Seconds. How the hell many?

Caesar hustled faster, listening to his own panting. Upstairs, Melaethia was abruptly silenced. He heard feet scrape the ladder rungs and knew 41 was coming down.

Good old 41 . . . tough as a gasket seal . . . always dependable in a fight whether he had holes in him or not. Caesar had seen Beaulieu frown and slip 41 another one of those green painkillers she kept locked like sacred treasure. As long as the chemicals held in 41's system, he would give Caesar good backup.

Halfway down . . . a yellow light was flashing in the ladder well, casting eerie shadows across Caesar's forearms as he climbed down past it. Life support was failing. The temperature was as hot as the Valu Desert and getting hotter. He sucked the beads of salty perspiration collecting in the corners of his mouth and kept hustling.

Seconds, Kelly had said. *Do it, or we're dead*.

Yusus. Nobody tried a manual jump these days. It was too complicated without the computers. One slip in timing and they'd be permanently bye-bye. Worry knotted Caesar's stomach. The hostage situation down here—a madman and a little kid—didn't make things any easier.

Caesar missed the last rung and hit the floor with a thud that jarred through his bootsoles. It was getting hard to breathe. The heat was far too intense.

He pressed his back to the wall and edged himself to the curve forming the base of the ladder well. He peered out, his forehead itching where a shot could drill it.

The corridor was empty. Caesar drew back, blowing out his breath in relief. He rubbed his forehead.

41 came off the ladder awkwardly, favoring his injured leg. His hair was matted to his head with sweat, and he looked like something a Jostic wouldn't eat.

"See him?" asked 41.

"No and we can't wait around for him to make the first move either." Caesar wiped his face with his sleeve. "We've got to get in position to hit that switch. One of us, anyway."

41 bared his teeth briefly in what, for him, served as a smile. He whipped himself into the corridor, and when nothing happened, he headed along it with one shoulder brushing the wall. Caesar followed fast, the ill-balanced blaster feeling awkward in his hand, going on adrenaline rush.

Just short of the teleport bay, 41 stopped so abruptly Caesar nearly ran into him. Side by side, they froze and listened intently. Caesar heard a whimper from the child. Dausal was muttering to himself in Saluk. There came the soft whine of a laser probe and the click of instrumentation.

Was he trying to repair the damage the Jostics had done to the teleport? Where did the boo-head think he was going to beam to?

Caesar gripped 41's shoulder, but 41 shook him off. Gesturing for Caesar to go ahead, 41 stepped into the open doorway of the teleport bay to provide Caesar with cover, and fired.

The shot went high because the child was right there in the way, standing between Dausal, who was crouched on the floor making repairs, and 41. The child cried out in wonder; Dausal yelled in fear. He skidded around on one knee, snatching the boy against him as a shield, and shot back.

Running past the doorway, Caesar thought the shot would catch 41, but it missed him by less than a centimeter and hit Caesar just above his left elbow.

Off balance, Caesar yelled in startlement and careened into the opposite wall. Then pain set in, fiery agony that flashed from his elbow to his shoulder. He choked on a breath, gritting his teeth to keep from screaming.

41 yanked him aside and a second bolt from Dausal's blaster smoked the wall where Caesar had been.

The near miss cleared the haziness from Caesar's brain. He staggered for balance. "Damn! Did you see him use the kid for cover? What a—"

"Go, Caesar," said 41. "I will hold him here. Hurry."

Caesar frowned, catching his wavering attention, and veered around to obey. The engine room was about twenty strides distant. It looked like a thousand. He clutched his arm, pinning it tight to his side against the pain. At least the blaster hadn't sheered it off at the elbow. At least there wasn't any blood. But it was a bad burn.

He felt suddenly cold and thought with relief that life support was finally compensating against that gain in temperature. But the yellow light was flashing over the engine room too. He sagged momentarily in the doorway, shivering, then felt the heat hit him in the face like a blasting inferno.

The engines were throbbing. Vibration came up through the floor and shook the walls. Behind him he heard percussion shots and knew Dausal had changed weapons. 41 wasn't returning much fire. But how could he shoot with a kid in the way?

On the wall, the comm spat and crackled with fitful bursts of static. No words were intelligible. Was Kelly giving the order?

Alarm burst within Caesar. He wrenched himself from the support of the wall and weaved through the cramped space toward the control panel. Data readouts were going crazy. The heat shimmered around Caesar, making him feel faint. He leaned on the console, caught himself slipping, and placed his palm upon the switch.

When to push? he wondered. *The comm's out. It's too hot for it to work.*

Instinct told him not to wait. The heat was deadly and sapping all coherence from him. The walls looked like they were melting.

"Burn up," he gasped aloud. "We're burning up."

He didn't understand how jumping into distort could save

them from photonic drive failure. But Kelly had given the order, and he would carry it out.

He coughed, the air scorching the tender lining of his nostrils and throat. With his final bit of strength, he pressed the switch.

For a moment nothing happened.

Caesar straightened painfully with a sense of failure. He hadn't waited for the order. It had to be timed precisely, and he'd screwed up.

Then the engines cried out. Caesar didn't know another word to use for the sound they made. It was an awful, wrenching noise of tortured machinery called on for more than its designed tolerance specifications. It was a screeching, labored revving accompanied by a rapidly worsening vibration that shook him off his feet.

He landed hard on his knees and stayed there, while the engines tore their own guts out to respond. A lurch sideways pitched him against the base of the console. It bumped his wounded arm where the burns were already blistering, and the resulting pain made him sag to the floor. He rolled there, clutching his arm, helpless in the sweating, sick oblivion of agony.

The shuddering lurch of the ship caught 41 unawares. Too late, he shifted his weight in an effort to keep his balance, but it put too much strain on his injured leg. He collapsed, and the tilt of the ship sent him rolling away from the protection of the wall.

Dausal's shot was wild, missing widely. 41 dragged himself into the teleport bay, hissing for breath when his bad leg was slammed against the doorway. Beaulieu's chemicals were still in his blood, and he was able to ignore the jolt of weakness that flowed down his thigh to his ankle.

Bracing his spine against a row of storage lockers, he sighted on Dausal, who was also changing position, but some instinct made the Salukan shift the boy into the line of fire again long enough to get under cover near the platform.

The child, at least, was not crying. His small face was scrunched up with fear, but he made no sound. His eyes looked enormous in his face.

Imprinting, 41 realized with annoyance. He wanted to snap Dausal's neck for filling the boy with such terror, but 41 forced himself to contain his emotions. At that age he himself had lacked parents to protect him. At that age he had not even yet been conscious of the Old Ones. He had fended for himself like a wild creature; naked, tiny, and always aware that something larger and stronger could eat him. His first memory was a fear memory: another child, older than him, being seized in the ruins near the tombs of the Old Ones and dragged off for food.

No shooting now. The ship was shaking like the end of the world. Clinging to his minimal cover, 41 lay upon the deck. It felt hot to his cheek. The air was too hot. Something very bad was happening to the ship. He had heard it in Kelly's voice.

The blaster in his hand blurred and became two. Then three. Then four. Edges blurred. He saw the spread of colors that told him they were entering distort. Badly. It should not happen like this.

The ship bumped up beneath him, tossing him into the air. He tried to catch himself in the fall and felt the strain in his wrist as he landed awkwardly. Dausal grunted, and the child cried out.

But 41 couldn't see them. The angles were wrong again. They were shaking too hard, shaking until he had to set his teeth together against the torture of that vibration. The lights went out. He felt another bump, not as rough this time, and then he was weightless.

He hated null-gravity and automatically reached out to hang onto something.

He was weightless, but he still sat on the floor.

Oddness. A feeling of pain in his chest near the new heart. He pressed his hand there and suddenly saw himself lying upon the floor, bleeding from the wound, with Kelly's anguished face above him. There were things he wanted to say to Kelly, things he had not yet said, but he was being sucked away as though down into a hole.

He saw a vision of water, rippling in concentric rings from the stones falling one by one into it.

Tears of the Old Ones.

He saw the mighty fist of 34 suspended above him, ready to

crash into his face. Heard 34's voice yelling at him in anger.
The ruined salm loader lay in pieces at his feet. He had tried to
repair it. He had failed.

He felt the blackness of the shipping crate enclosing him,
felt the squirming, bony body of another child pressed in with
him. The crate was too small for the both of them. He couldn't
breathe, and the other child was kicking him. 41 felt savage
anger. He struck out in retaliation, again and again, until the
other boy lay still, whimpering, and did not crowd him.

He was in a place of machinery whirring in a comforting
way. A place of whiteness. Other babies cooed, moist and
plump and contented. He cooed along with them and waved his
arms. He lay in pleasant softness, and the mist falling upon his
face made him blink. But the mist was warm and also pleasant.
He stuck out his tongue and squealed, and the other babies
squealed too.

He . . .

Slam came, and it felt like being hurled through glass. The
shock of impact, the sudden, giddy sense of motion that was
too fast, the feel of gravity again.

41 opened his eyes. They were wet. He thought with tears,
but he did not know what he wept for.

Then he remembered that he had gone backwards in time,
gone almost all the way back to his beginning, when he would
have know the full truth of who he was for the first time.
Known it from himself, and without lies.

But he had not gone far enough. And now he would never
know.

He lifted an unsteady hand and wiped his eyes.

Sitting up was difficult. He felt groggy and lethargic. His
mind wandered. He had forgotten his purpose for being here.
Then he heard a whimpering sound. Picking up his weapon, 41
crawled cautiously toward it.

He found Dausal huddled with his arms drawn tightly around
the little boy. The boy lay limp, his eyes closed. A tiny pulse
fluttered near the corner of one eye. Dausal's dark head was
bowed. He kept making that small sound of grief over and over
again.

41 tipped back his head. Dausal's eyes were closed. 41

thumped him. Dausal opened his eyes slowly and tried to focus. 41 took the child, and the small warm body cuddled against his chest in a way he found pleasant.

Dausal's weapon lay forgotten on the deck beside him. 41 kicked it beyond reach, then limped to the comm.

He did not want to talk yet. He had come through an experience too great to be thrust away so soon, but there were things to be done. He could not afford to be kind to himself. 41 reached out to the comm, hesitated, then pushed the button.

"41 to Kelly," he said. His voice was hoarse, and he swallowed painfully. "41 to Kelly. Come in."

After a very long while, Kelly answered. His voice sounded weak over the comm—weak and tired. "What's your status?"

"I have Dausal and the boy," said 41. He shifted the child over his shoulder, where the weight was less heavy. "I don't know about Caesar yet."

"We have the Salukans confined up here," said Kelly. "Secure Dausal immediately. Oh, and 41?"

"Yes?"

"Did you get us through that jump?"

41 heard the warmth returning to Kelly's voice and felt anew the peculiar bond between them; a bond that made them friends although they had little to base a friendship on, a bond that made them take risks for each other because they could not do otherwise.

"No," said 41. "Your praise will be for Caesar."

He was smiling as he spoke. Then from the corner of his eye he saw a shadow loom up over him. 41 tried to turn, but he was hampered by the boy he held.

Something heavy crashed down upon his skull. His vision blacked on him, but he still retained enough consciousness to know he had not yet fallen. He reached out blindly, fighting to hang on, fighting to stay awake. Vaguely he felt the boy's weight sliding from his shoulder. Something banged into his skull a second time, in the same place, and pain split through his head.

It was the last thing he knew before he hit the floor.

11

There are three sources of slavery: cowardice, guilt, and love. The most powerful of these is love.

—from the Sacred Scrolls, VII

Kelly slowly walked the blackened, scarred corridor between his quarters and sickbay. He was supposed to be sleeping, but he was too exhausted for sleep. His body ached with fatigue; his mind could not rest.

Quietly he entered the sickbay, gazing around at the softly humming machinery of support and regeneration. Beaulieu sat at her desk with her head down in sleep, one dark hand still resting upon the keyboard. The vid screen glowed upon her face. Kelly smiled and stepped past her without a sound.

In the treatment room Caesar lay upon one of the bunks, his injured arm encased in a re-gen tube. Fluids and nutrients passed from the main re-gen unit to the tube, healing the burned tissue while he slept. Kelly paused to gaze down at that freckled face, looking vulnerable and pale, red hair standing on end as usual. Kelly felt an overwhelming urge to grip Caesar's shoulder and say, "Well, done." There was no question that Caesar had saved their lives.

Kelly walked on and stood a while gazing somberly at the life support capsule where Ouoji lay stretched out on her side, ear flap slackly half-opened, fur matted, eyes shut and sunk into her skull. Ouoji had saved their lives too, for she had given them the chance they needed to overwhelm their captors. Some might say she had nearly cost them their lives, but Ouoji knew this ship as well or better than any of them. Better than Siggerson, who even now was shut away in his quarters, his eyes haunted with embarrassment and humiliation. Ouoji had known when she sabotaged the *Sabre* that it could withstand the abuse.

Pressing his palm upon the window of the capsule, Kelly whispered, "Live," making it a prayer.

Then he dropped his hand and moved to the bunk where 41 lay unconscious. Dried blood still crusted his hair. A drug patch was attached to his throat. The monitors relayed data on him. Kelly read them although he did not know what 41's normal heart rate or blood pressure was supposed to be.

He smiled down at his friend, glad to have him alive. When Kelly had walked into the teleport bay and seen 41 lying there in his own blood, he had thought the worst.

But they were all alive, his squad. Kelly was thankful, although this situation was far from over yet.

Time to either sleep or plan. Kelly made his way from the sickbay, as quiet as a ghost, and was almost to the door of his quarters when he heard a faint noise behind him.

Startled, he glanced back and saw 41 leaning against the wall of the corridor, holding his head as though it ached.

Kelly went to him at once. "41, what are you doing out of bed? You can't go wandering around."

41's pupils were contracted to points. He looked at Kelly as though his vision was not quite tracking yet. "What is it here?" he said, none too coherently. "Teleport . . . Dausal."

Kelly frowned and gripped his forearm. "Back to bed. You need rest."

"No, Dausal—"

"Old Dausal gave you a pretty bad knock on the head. I know your skull is as tough as pyrillium, but Beaulieu will have a fit if she finds you wandering around."

41 planted his feet and would not allow Kelly to lead him back. He met Kelly's eyes this time with more cognizance. "Trouble. Dausal . . . hit me."

"Yes."

"Still has the boy?"

"Yes." With a sigh, Kelly gave in. "He teleported before we could get down to help you."

"Then he is dead. And the boy is dead." 41 frowned fiercely. "I do not hear Melaethia grieving."

"They aren't dead. We're orbiting a planet. Not a very habitable one, but it has some breathable air. Dausal's got a distress beacon going down there, but he'll keep until we're rested enough to go after him."

41 tipped his head back against the wall and sighed. "Melaethia was right. He is mad. And he could hurt the boy."

Kelly looked at him, waiting to hear more.

"Dausal used the boy as a shield—"

"To keep you from firing."

"For self-protection." 41 shook his head, then winced. "The line he walks is very fine."

"Then we have a difficult hostage situation," said Kelly, not liking it. "But surely he realizes that without the boy on the throne, he has no chance of restitution into their society. Unless . . . if the boy dies, can the girls inherit?"

41 snorted. "No. Think, Kelly. A female rule the Empire? They do not even understand why we give our females weapons."

"Then we have to depend on Dausal to not hurt the boy."

"When we attack, he will feel endangered," said 41. "That could snap his mind. He may kill the boy just to thwart us."

Kelly frowned into the distance. "We must not let that happen. We've botched this whole mission from the first. I won't let it end with an innocent child's death."

"Sometimes," said 41, "your will is not God's."

"What's that supposed to mean?" said Kelly sharply.

"I do not speak in double layers, Kelly. You understand me. Dausal will do whatever he decides to do. If we are swift and clever, we will get him. But the child could already be dead. Then is that our blame? Is it yours more than mine, when I turned my back to him and let him strike me?"

Seeing the guilt in 41's eyes, Kelly let his own anger fade. "You're right," he said at last, reluctantly. "Time we both got some sleep. We've a lot to do when the sun comes up on Dausal's side of that planet."

He took 41's arm to help him back into the sickbay, but again 41 did not move.

"No, Kelly," he said. "I will see the woman now."

Kelly's brows went up. "She's asleep, sedated. Beaulieu had to give her something to calm those hysterics."

41 nodded. "Still, I will see her. When she awakens, I will talk to her."

"I'm not sure she needs to know," began Kelly.

"She bore the child. It is her right. You and I, Kelly, have no rights to fight her brother for possession of her son. We are stepping across Salukan codes. It is necessary to take care."

"But we're on her side!" said Kelly in exasperation. "We're trying to help her."

"From an Earther standpoint, yes, but she is Salukan and will always be Salukan, no matter how long she exiles herself. There is much confusion within her mind. If she cannot resolve it, she will return to Salukan ways and hate us. We could create a great enemy to the Alliance."

"I see," said Kelly. He sighed. "Do you want me to go with you?"

For the first time a glint of amusement showed in 41's eyes. "On leave, Kelly, when you finally had the long-awaited date with Cassandra Caliban, did you take me along?"

Heat burned in Kelly's face at the gentle rebuke. He dropped his gaze, frowned, and said, "But that was different. Uh, you—"

"How different?" said 41, showing even more amusement.

Aware that his face was probably red, Kelly glared at him. "A short time ago, you declared Melaethia strictly off limits, persona non grata, the last female in the galaxy you would even consider."

41 snorted. "I did. She is young and arrogant. She is much trained in the arts of seduction and she has felt vein-burn only once. But her fertility time has passed. She is no longer trying to manipulate males. Now she is only a mother."

"I see," said Kelly. No matter how societies tried to repattern themselves, some old ways still clung. 41 was insulted as long as Melaethia was making the moves. Now that she'd stopped, he was interested. Kelly dropped his gaze, not wanting 41 to see what he was thinking. "Well, uh, go ahead."

41 said nothing more, but his yellow eyes were ironical as they watched Kelly enter his quarters. Only then did 41 leave the support of the wall and go to Melaethia.

She slept the black, dreamless sleep of drugs. Then the blackness was pierced by a thought. She came awake with a start, conscious of her mind clearing, then aware of a stranger's hand upon her face.

Reaching up, she clasped a sturdy wrist and pulled the hand away. Opening her eyes, she saw 41's face hanging in the shadows above her. Even as the first emotions registered within her, he moved away and stood at least a meter from her couch.

He did not speak. She felt her own heartbeat like a slow, steady drum within her abdomen. She felt the warmth of her own femininity, still alive beneath the coldness of her fears and her agony as a mother.

Her daughters slept, undisturbed.

The air smelled of him. He had been here a long time. She frowned at the chron, but could not figure out how many hours had passed.

"It is almost time to go," he said in Saluk. His voice made a harsh whisper that slid across the smooth texture of her mind. She imagined the strength of his hands, bruising her with passion.

She said, also in a whisper, "Why did you wake me like this? Did you come to mock me?"

"We will fight your brother soon," he said.

He used the warrior inflection on the word fight. She knew this man would kill Dausal if he could. Old confusions rose within her.

"My son still lives," she said. "He has not killed my son. He will not kill him unless you force his hand."

"Do you then wish us to go and leave Dausal on this planet? Do you wish to abandon your son? He will be Pharaon without your guidance."

"I shall have no guidance!" she burst out. "I shall live secluded, walled away in silence where none will speak to me or see me. They cannot draw the blood of the Mother of Pharaon, but there are other ways of death. Why not let him go without me? He is lost to me as he is."

"A baby, not yet named," said 41, and his contempt was like a blow. "Imprinted with fear. Imprinted by a madman. Dominated perhaps by this madman who is your kinsman. Abused and made an eager puppet of those who will scorn his weakness. He will learn to please them. He will be a small, sickly, cowed thing, despised by those who wield true power. And when his purpose is done, they will give him a sickness to be rid of him, and the dynasty will shift into new hands."

The scenario he painted was true. Terrified of it, she gave a muffled cry into her palms.

"He could be strong," she said, more to convince herself than 41. "He could make his name ring upon the stones of the Defended City."

"He is too young," said 41. "They will have him too young. His identity is not yet formed. You know this."

Grief twisted within her. "I know it."

"Then we will fight Dausal and take back the boy."

She lifted her face and gazed at him through the gloom. "Is that a request for my permission?"

"Yes."

This tall, aloof man with his blond mane and his savage eyes. Half-tamed. Lacking either House or breeding. Lacking manners, yet able to caress gently with those killing hands if he but would. It was forbidden to feel blood-call for an Earther, yet 41 was only half Earther, therefore only half forbidden. Excitement shivered within her, aroused by his request. For him to ask anything of her was to humble him and make him hers.

She delayed answering, enjoying the superiority he gave her. Did he realize it? Did he know Salukan custom?

She leaned forward and studied him, and saw by his stillness that he did know.

"Kelly is the leader here," she said. "Why did he not come and ask this of me?"

41 took a step forward, and she knew by his smell that he was angered. "Kelly is a warrior of great position. He will not be humbled by an exiled female of no worth."

"And so you have come to ask for him?"

"I have come."

"You understand our customs well," she said. "You have honored me."

He said nothing.

"Your companions have fought long and hard for my son. That honors him. Dausal hates him, hates him as he hates me. I do not know if the Empire sent Dausal after us to bring us back or to kill us. I am afraid my son will die."

41 still said nothing.

She realized he was not going to help her make the decision. He had asked, but she suspected even if she denied permission they would still go and fight Dausal.

"How many of you against my brother?" she asked.

41 shrugged.

"All of you?" she cried. "Is that fair? Is that justice?"

"Do you want your son to live, or your brother?"

"What choice is that?" she said angrily. "My father is dead. Dausal is my last kinsman. All the family I have—"

"You have your children."

"I do not want my brother to die. Not by my order."

41 bared his teeth. "Guilt is a difficult burden. You must live with the consequences of your actions for many years, Mela-ethia. Sometimes all your life."

"Do you accuse me for what I did?" she said with a gasp. "What right have you to judge me?"

"You judge yourself," he said. "I do not have to."

It was true. She pressed her face against her palms, hot with memories and the tormenting guilt that would not leave her. "He would have killed me," she whispered. "The Pharaon would not release me from vein-burn. I had to use the dagger for separation. I had to."

"You did not have to go to the Pharaon," said 41. "That was your pride."

"It was my gift to the Alliance," she retorted. "Would you be here to protect me if I did not have Nefir's children?"

"No."

"Ah." Smugly she sat back, and only then saw the trap he'd boxed her into.

"Nefir's son can stay within the Alliance's protection, or he can go to the Empire. While he is young, you must decide for him. Will we fight Dausal?"

She knew she must agree, knew she had no choice, hadn't had a choice ever. But still she resisted. She wanted something in exchange from 41, something he did not intend to give her. But need she punish herself and her son just because she wanted to punish 41?

A long sigh escaped her. "You may fight Dausal," she said, resenting each word.

41 inclined slightly and turned to go.

"Wait!" she called.

He paused and she left her couch to stand before him in her thin sleeping robe. Her time of fertility was almost past, but its drive still made her hunger. She wanted the reassurance of a man's touch upon her. She wanted to know that she was still desirable to someone.

"It is my turn to ask," she whispered in a shaking voice. She fumbled with the clasp of her robe and shrugged it off her shoulders to fall in a heap upon the floor. She faced him, shaking slightly, vulnerable, aching.

He glanced at the door, and she thought he was going to leave. Rage and humiliation battled within her, then he walked toward her with a purpose that made her breath tangle in her throat.

The callouses on his palms snagged her smooth skin as he ran his hands up her arms to her shoulders and pulled her near. She embraced him, her blood surging hot and ready, and found him all hard bone and muscle beneath his clothes. She wanted his clothes off. She wanted to sink her teeth into his skin and taste his blood.

He picked her up and put her upon the couch. He was all shadow and indistinction above her. She heard his breathing over the thrumming of her heart. He captured her roving hands and held them between his. He kissed her fingers gently, then touched her face.

Like a shock she felt his mind within hers, so cold it made her shiver. And the fever within her increased, making her body quiver without control.

"41," she said, her voice crying for him. She tried to invade his mind in return, but he kept her out. "Please. Please!"

"Hush!" he said harshly. "Listen to me."

His fingertips shifted on her cheekbone, and she felt him play along her nerve endings in a way that brought such a swift burst of pleasure she groaned aloud. He knew the love ways of Solan, goddess of fertility and marriage, ways that were kept secret from almost everyone. Not even the trainers within the Court of Women had known this. They had spoken of it with longing, but they had not known. How, then, did this man have such mysteries in his keeping?

Her questions faded as he touched her again and again, finding precise points and sending his mind through her in ways that brought explosions of exquisite ecstasy. She felt as though she were spinning off the edge of all reality. She had never known such heat, such swift exhilaration, such searing torment in her limbs, such dizzy sensations within her womb. She called out, locked in vein-burn, locked in something beyond vein-burn, and her cry would have marked conception had he been with her physically.

And when she could endure no more, when her heart was going too fast, her breath became too jerky, her body singing beyond what it could bear, and she felt the first stir of self-preservation within her, he was aware of it and brought her down gently, gently, his mind releasing the tensions within her, his mind calming her by steady degrees until she lay drenched with sweat and exhausted.

He released her hands and she lifted them to her face. She was weeping. She had never known such happiness, and yet it was not complete.

"Why?" she whispered, wiping away tears only to have more come.

He took her wet hand and slipped it inside his uniform tunic to press her fingers against his heart. She felt the warmth of his skin and the steady rhythm within his chest.

"My heart belongs elsewhere," he whispered.

She heard the strain in his voice and knew he was not as detached as he seemed.

"Listen," he said.

His mind touched hers lightly. This time Melaethia concentrated, and she saw an image of an Earther woman, tall and gray-eyed.

"Kevalyn," whispered Melaethia, wondering who she was. "Is that her name?"

"It is her name," he said.

"You have not shared with her?"

"No."

"You have not given her what you gave to me tonight?"

41 glanced away without answer. His longing flooded into her. Melaethia withdrew her hand from his tunic and knew she had intruded upon private pain.

"Why do you not tell her?" she asked.

He bowed his head. "I cannot. She is . . . I am not enough."

Tenderness filled Melaethia. Oh, if only he knew that he was more than enough. And she envied this Kevalyn woman, wherever she might be. "In her eyes you may also be special," said Melaethia gently. "Is that not what is important?"

"Perhaps. But it is not as easy as you think."

"You must try."

He shook his head.

"Because you are half?" Melaethia said hesitantly.

He stood up as though he would walk away, but then he remained standing beside her. She stared at his thigh and longed to touch it, yet dared not.

"I am half," he said bitterly. "That makes me sterile. You should have realized that, Melaethia, when you longed to conceive again."

"It is no longer important to me," she said, afraid of him in that moment of bitterness. "You shared with me beautifully. I want to thank you for the gift of Solan—"

"Hush." It was a command, spoken curtly. "Do not ask me questions. My past is not for you to know."

Her eyes fell. "Ahe," she said humbly.

For a moment longer he stood there, rigid and angry, then

his mood changed again. He set his hand lightly upon her head, his palm cradling the back of her skull.

"I lied to Kelly in order to come here," he said. "I have let you know things that are important secrets. You have power over me now."

She smiled to herself, aware that that also was a lie. 41 granted power to no one. When his loyalty ended, he left.

"You are polite," she said. "It is not necessary. I shall not betray your secrets."

He nodded once and left her. She ached all over, and yet she was contented. Her fears for Dausal and her son were gone.

Realizing the absence of those fears made her sit up and frown. He had done more to her than she realized. He had used her own passions to enslave her. He had manipulated her sympathy. He had told her secrets that might or might not be true. He had left her short of satiation, yet made her content with it.

He had prepared her well for Dausal's death on the morrow, for she would not swear vengeance if it happened. She would not throw her sympathies back to the Empire. Even the thought of doing so made a sudden sweat of weakness go through her.

She realized that 41 had conditioned her while he made love to her. He had awakened such passion that her mind had been completely open to whatever he wanted to do with it. In the future he would have only to look into her eyes and touch her mind, and she would be an instant slave to his wishes.

That frightened her. She had been a fool to give such power over herself to a man like him.

Yet 41 was not ambitious. He would not use her and her son. Or would he?

12

Ambition is like a deadly serpent. It coils. It waits. It strikes.
                    —*School Manual, teachings of Hithmal*

Dawn over an unnamed planet in an unwanted system. A dawn of rosy tints and long shadows. A plain of jagged rock outcroppings and dust. Dry, scentless air. Nothing growing. Nothing alive but the stir of wind drawing patterns in the sand.

Kelly, 41, and Phila teleported down into a sheltered pocket of rock pillars, copper red in hue and thrusting tall into the sky. Kelly glanced around and called in while Phila checked their bearings on a hand-scanner.

She should have been on the *Sabre*, helping Siggerson make repairs. The *Sabre* had suffered extensive internal damage. It was questionable whether she could continue to produce enough power to maintain her orbit. Siggerson had broken out the repair drones to assist him, and Beaulieu was helping. Caesar was still laid up due to complications with his injured arm. 41 shouldn't have been down here either. The effects of over-exertion showed. His face looked grainy, and he was still limping heavily. Kelly, however, needed him and Kelly had overridden Beaulieu's protests.

"Dausal's that way, Commander," said Phila, pointing. "Siggerson set us down precisely a quarter mile from his position. I have two life signs, and that beacon is signalling steadily."

Kelly glanced at the pale green sky. "Hope it doesn't mean a Salukan battlecruiser is nearby," he muttered.

41 took out a pair of binocs and surveyed the landscape. Kelly did the same. The binocs had over a kilometer in range, but broken country like this diminished range severely. They had low ridges and shallow gullies to cross. The boulders and loose shale would make going slow.

Kelly glanced doubtfully at 41, who was leaning against one of the rock pillars with his weight off his injured leg. 41 had trained his binocs south, in the opposite direction of where Dausal waited. He watched something, every line of his body intent.

Unease prickled along the back of Kelly's neck. "What is it?" he asked, making Phila glance that way too. "Do you see something?"

"No." 41 kept the binocs trained a moment longer before lowering them. "For a moment I thought so, but there is nothing."

With a hostage involved, Kelly had opted not to bring along their die-hards. He drew his bi-muzzle Maxell pistol and double-checked the action. "Everyone's pistol set on stun?" he asked.

Both Phila and 41 nodded.

"Good. Make sure it stays that way. I don't want the boy hurt from a passing shot."

Already the sun was climbing into the sky. The temperature climbed with it. Kelly finished his checks. He hated hostage recovery. It was tricky, even when only adults were involved. No matter how much training you went through, it was hard not to let emotions become involved. And emotions were distractions that could get you killed.

Kelly glanced at 41 again and made a decision. "41, I want you to stay here."

41's yellow eyes swung his way. Kelly didn't give him a chance to speak. "Keep your comm line open at all times. We may need backup, and I'd prefer you fresh."

For a moment there was silence. At the best of times 41 was

touchy about any doubt cast upon his fighting abilities. Phila stared at him warily, and Kelly did too.

But 41's gaze shifted without any change in expression. "I will wait," he said in a toneless voice.

Kelly let out his breath in relief. That was milder than he'd expected. 41 must be hurting quite a lot to give up the chance for a piece of the action.

"Come on, Phila," said Kelly. "Let's get this over with."

From his vantage point atop a small ridge, Dausal lay in the shadow of a split boulder and watched Kelly and the small female trudge away toward his trap. Dausal smiled to himself and rubbed his hands together. His strategy was working well. How easy to predict the actions of these Earthers. They fought like demons, but they thought no better than an onole burrower. Tunneling here, tunneling there, blind to everything except their own sense of purpose.

The half-breed, however, stayed put. Squinting inside protective goggles, Dausal watched him a moment and decided he was no threat either. Actually it was ideal for the Earthers to split up. That would make them easier to capture.

Turning, Dausal slid down the ridge, taking care to raise no dust, and hobbled rapidly along the edge of a shallow gully for a short distance before jumping down into the bottom of it. Gradually the sides rose until they were even with his head, then above it. The sand in the bottom was very deep and coarse, making walking difficult. Dausal panted as he hurried.

His camp awaited him around a bend. There had not been time to gather more than minimum emergency equipment before escaping the ship. Most of what he had he'd been carrying in his pockets. Although small, the force field he'd erected was serving its purpose well. It surrounded the boy, who looked up at Dausal's arrival and hissed irritably.

The boy hungered, and there was no food for him. Dausal knew the danger of that, but rescue would come soon.

Dausal watched the boy a moment, looking for resemblance to Melaethia in that small face. But the lines were all Juvanne. He would look much like Nefir when he grew. Envy tightened in Dausal's chest. This wretched child would soon hold the

Empire in his tiny hands. This piece of his sister's flesh would make Dausal incline and grovel. Dausal could feel gorge rise in his throat at the very thought. He controlled himself, breathing hard.

He wanted to kill this child, and the boy knew it. He watched Dausal, black eyes wary. Perhaps even a little afraid. The next best thing to killing the boy was to dominate him.

A rush of excitement went through Dausal. It was forbidden. Muetet, the man who had taken him from the mines and set him free to carry out this mission, had made that prohibition clear. Only Muetet was to touch the child. The House of Toth meant to wrest ultimate power from the House of Juvanne with this new Pharaon on the throne.

Dausal's fingers curled in a surge of old hatred. Was it right that anyone but this boy's uncle dominate him? No, Muetet was mistaken there. Muetet wanted the power for himself, but that power should belong to Dausal. As for the half-breed's claim of dominance, that was only a lie.

The boy, as though sensing the direction of Dausal's thoughts, whimpered softly, then hissed and backed away. Defiant black eyes. How little they knew of training and subjugation.

Dausal's own breath hissed in his throat. He spoke a non-word to the boy, making the command tone whip through his voice, and the boy flinched. Dausal laughed. It would be sweet to break the spirit of this brat.

A noise in the distance stopped him from entering the tiny area guarded by the force field. Blinking, Dausal froze and listened hard. The wind perhaps. Or something else.

He did not trust the Earthers. More of them might have teleported down.

For a moment he felt uncertainty, even fear. His plan must not fail now. But this place of concealment could not be found. The force field's power wave negated ship's sensors, as did the field he wore about his own person. They could not be detected by the scanners which Kelly carried.

Dausal shifted his stance, relaxing as he heard nothing further. He thought of Kelly, hurrying toward the life signs which were produced mechanically by a little device left as bait for Dausal's trap.

Time to close the trap around Kelly. Time to show this upstart Earther what a true Salukan warrior could do. The boy could wait. There would be plenty of opportunities to deal with him later.

Grinning to himself, Dausal turned to the steep side of the gully and fitted his hands and toes into shallow niches which he'd carved there last night. He climbed out, grunting with the effort, and had to squirm upon his belly a little before making it onto the top. He rolled over onto his side, and his force field crackled sharply at a stress point from the pressure. At once it cut off to avoid shorting. Dausal sat up, slapping the dust from his sleeves and leggings, and boosted the power gain a notch to compensate. The field reactivated at once.

Drawing his weapon, he headed after Kelly and the female. Once they were caught, he would circle back and kill the half-breed. Then he would dominate the boy.

41's sense of restlessness increased. He had felt something off from the first moment of materialization, but since it was not always useful to announce his hunches to Kelly, he had said nothing.

His hand-scanner said Dausal was a quarter mile north of this position. His senses told him something watched from the south. 41 climbed stiffly to his feet and limped around. Each step sent pain through the entire length of his leg, and his head throbbed mercilessly. He had not told Beaulieu this because he did not want Kelly to leave him on the ship. But now he feared his own weakness would slow him down too much.

He glanced south once, then gazed steadily west. His mind attuned itself in the direction of the watcher, and he waited. He had the long patience of the hunter, and after several moments of inner silence, he picked up a glimmer of a mind. Not enough to recognize, and it came and went so swiftly he might have imagined it.

But 41 did not often imagine things, and he did not speculate now. Drawing his pistol, he reset the charge level from stun to lethal, then pretended to touch the comm on his wristband as though receiving orders. He headed due west for about a hundred meters until he could safely duck into the cover of a series of small washes. Then he circled south.

In ten minutes he found tracks, long skid marks down a ridge that told him where the watcher had hidden. 41 studied the gully edge, finding few marks among the stones. But within a short distance, deep indentations were found in the sandy bottom of the gully. The watcher had jumped down there. His tracks were plain upon the sand. Uneven, one foot dragging.

41's mouth tightened with satisfaction. Dausal.

41 scanned quickly and read nothing. He put the instrument away with a scowl. It was of little use to him at the best of times. He knew that a man inside a force field would not register. Dausal could be lurking nearby. These tracks were very fresh.

Instead of jumping into the gully, 41 stayed up on the edge, and kept a constant watch in all directions as he hurried. A faint hum ahead caught his attention. He dropped to his knees and slewed himself into cover.

Waiting there for several moments brought no shout of discovery, no sound of movement ahead. Cautiously 41 peered around the stone. On his belly he crawled to the edge of the gully and looked in. Nothing except the tracks.

He turned his head right and squinted up at the ridge over him. It was a good place for an ambush. His spine tingled uncomfortably, feeling exposed.

Crawling on a short distance farther, he peered down again. This time he found himself gazing into the black eyes of Melaethia's son. The child stared at him without a sound, then it lifted its hand and waved in the aimless way of a baby. A low force field held him penned up.

41 drew his prong and stabbed the small receptor nodule. A vicious series of sparks spat at him, scorching his hand. He let go of the hilt just in time to avoid electrocution, and the entire field blazed and wavered before shorting out. The smell of acrid smoke boiled into the air.

Blinking, 41 eyed the blackened remains of his prong and realized just how close he'd come to crisping himself along with it. Perhaps Phila was right about circuit differences.

Perhaps a stab was not always the wisest way to short out a system.

No matter now. He'd accomplished it. Carefully he lowered himself into the gully, favoring his leg. Once down, he fought off a wave of dizziness and regarded the child, who was sitting on the sand, dirt-streaked and pale. The child held up his hands to 41 and began to whimper.

It was a hunger cry. 41 knelt beside him and unwrapped a ration bar. He broke off a small piece, too small to choke on, and gave it to the boy, who promptly spit it out.

41 indulged this defiance by ignoring it. After a few seconds, the boy picked up the bit of food and ate it, dirt and all. 41 gave him another piece, frowning.

It did not make sense. Dausal had been scanned elsewhere, and this child too. Yet the child was here, concealed, and Dausal . . .

With a muttered curse, 41 whipped out his scanner and stood up. He aimed it north, tapping it when the data readouts did not come fast enough. Yes, there were the two Salukan life signs. And there came Kelly and Phila, approaching close to the spot now.

Alarm went through 41. He tapped his comm. "Kelly!" he said urgently. "It's a trap. Fall back!"

"This is Kelly," came the reply. "What is your—"

Phila's scream cut across Kelly's voice. Kelly shouted, then the comm went dead.

41 tapped it in rising desperation, but he could get no answer. Dausal's trap had sprung.

"41 to ship. Come in!"

"Siggerson here."

"There is trouble," said 41 curtly. "Can you pinpoint Kelly and Phila and teleport them out?"

The pause while Siggerson checked seemed interminable. 41 mentally cursed the pilot while he waited with increasing tension, longing to stretch Siggerson with rope and make him scream while he learned the consequences of not acting quickly.

"Not possible," said Siggerson, sounding concerned. "I can't pinpoint them on the scanners. They aren't picking up in

the teleport readouts either. What the devil is going on? 41?
41?"

But 41 cut the line without reply. If Siggerson could not
help, then it was a waste of time to explain the situation to him.

41 scooped up the boy and set him on the gully edge, then
climbed out the way Dausal had. The tracks were easy to find.
41's eyes burned, and he forgot his own weariness and pain in
the need for vengeance. Dausal would not escape him again,
not for this. Not if he had to hunt the miserable Salukan across
the breadth of this planet for the rest of his life. Not if he had
to chase him across the galaxy.

It was sworn.

When 41's call came across the comm, Kelly paused with
his leg braced upon a rock and his back to a steep hillside and
let Phila climb ahead of him. Dausal's camp was just around
the bend. Both of them had their weapons in hand and were
moving with absolute quiet.

41's voice over the comm shattered that quiet with hoarse
urgency. The warning came just as Phila screamed.

Forgetting 41, Kelly whipped around and ran back the way
they'd just come, leaving the narrow trail and climbing straight
up the hillside. Whatever had caught her wasn't going to catch
him as well.

He crested the hill on his belly, breathing hard, and found
himself staring down at a small clearing littered with the ruins
of some kind of building made of dressed stone. It was the last
thing he expected to see on this empty planet, but right now he
wasn't interested in the architecture of vanished civilizations.
Resting upon a floor slab was the beacon signal and a smaller
broadcast device. Of Dausal and the child, there was no sign.

A trap indeed.

Still looking for Phila, Kelly scrambled down the hill toward
the camp, staying alert for attack. Then he saw her, pinned
upon an invisible force wall with her limbs splayed in frozen
agony. She was caught in an unseen web. She did not move.
She did not make a sound. From this distance he could not see
if she were dead.

Kelly backed up, looking around. There was an air of unseen

menace in this place. Although he refused to be spooked by it, the hair on his neck was standing and he felt the almost overwhelming need to run.

He touched his comm, and from overhead heard a crackling whiz of a sound. Instinct more than anything else made Kelly yank at the wristband. He got it loose just as a bolt of energy zapped the wristband and pinned it in mid-air. Kelly felt a horrifying tingle in his wrist and arm, and jerked free just in time to avoid a lightning-display of energy which whipped through the air next to him.

A split-second slower and he would have been caught in that energy web just like Phila. Kelly stumbled back and took cover, aware that if he activated his pistol, it would also draw the web to trap him.

Inside, he was still shaken from how close he'd come, and beneath that ran anger. Dausal was full of nasty little surprises. But Kelly had had enough of coping with them.

He drew his prong, snapping out all three blades. Somewhere in these silent, eerie rocks, Dausal waited like a spider. When he came, Kelly would get him.

On the *Sabre*, Siggerson wiped sweat from his face and swore long and loudly.

Beaulieu looked at him in alarm. "Get 41 back on," she said. "Now, Siggerson—"

"I can't! He's not transmitting," said Siggerson. He glared at her, feeling helpless and hating it.

"You've got to do something," said Beaulieu. "They're in trouble. I'll go down."

He caught her arm before she could leave the bridge. "Don't be a fool," he said. "You can't help them."

"I might."

"What are you trying to do, Doctor? Play heroine?"

"What about yourself, Siggerson?" she retorted. "Still without your nerve?"

It was a dirty blow. She knew as much as all of them how deeply he regretted his behavior before. He still felt raw with humiliation, for he had never known before that he was a coward, that he even had the capacity for cowardice. He had always believed that he could deal with any crisis, but he had found out otherwise.

He stepped back from her, his mouth tight.

Her expression changed. "Oh, hell, Siggerson. I'm sorry, but I won't sit up here helplessly as long as there's something we can do to help them."

It wasn't enough of an apology, but he nodded stiffly in acceptance. "Why don't you try to get 41 back? At least he's still registering."

"Right."

Beaulieu moved briskly to the communications station. But while she was making the call, she stopped in mid-word.

Immersed again in his repairs, Siggerson ignored her. Try as he might he could not get the conversion generators to reactivate. Without them, they were going to have a decayed orbit in a matter of hours.

He thought about crashing, of having to beam down with salvaged equipment and a beacon. They might be stranded here for months, years perhaps. The planet was marginally inhabitable. Sensors had reported some plant and primitive animal life on the other hemisphere, but the water teemed with toxic bacteria. He rubbed his eyes, so weary his head buzzed. He did not want the others to blame him for this as well, and they would.

"Siggerson," said Beaulieu and her voice sounded very odd. "What is this?"

He glanced up with irritation. "What?"

"Look at it."

"Beaulieu, I'm busy—"

"You'd better look at this."

This time her tone got through to him. With a sense of foreboding, he went to her station. The scanners showed an approaching blip.

Siggerson went cold with alarm. For a moment he panicked, then with a wrench of his own will he steadied and forced himself to think. Reaching over Beaulieu's shoulder, he called up data.

"What is it?" she whispered, as intent upon the readouts as he. "A ship?"

"Enemy ship," he said and his voice was so controlled it sounded wooden. "Salukan configuration."

"It's big. A battlecruiser?"

"No. Not that big." He called up registry data and frowned. "Privately owned. Non-military vessel. What the—"

"Dausal's beacon," said Beaulieu, slamming her palm down upon the console. "Can't we shoot that thing to bits, or something?"

"Too late. They've homed in on it at this range."

Beaulieu looked up at him. "If we've spotted them, have they spotted us?"

"Unknown. A private craft could have all kinds of capabilities. Her long-range detectors may be to military specifications, or they may not."

"We'd better count on the worst," said Beaulieu.

Siggerson nodded. "Agreed. Perhaps I can get the waver shield to . . ."

His voice trailed off. Not on their low battery reserves. Not unless he got that conversion generator operating again so that they could utilize the light scoop. "Why didn't they let *me* sabotage her?" he said out loud. "I could have reduced the damage."

"Never mind that," she said. "What are we going to do about this ship? We can't just sit here."

He started to tell her that there wasn't anything they could do, that they had no choice but to sit here because the ship couldn't move, but he held the words back. He wasn't going to be accused of whining again.

"Notify 41," he said.

"What the hell can 41 do about it?"

"Maybe he can still reach Kelly," said Siggerson in exasperation. He turned back to his repairs.

"Is that all the suggestions you have?" shouted Beaulieu.

His grip on the laser probe whitened. For an instant he thought about throwing it at her, but he controlled the urge as a childish, stupid one. "That's all I have," he said coldly. "You could try—"

"You are shouting," said Melaethia's voice, startling both of them. She stood in the doorway, hugging herself, looking young and worried. "Is there more trouble?"

"More trouble," said Siggerson with a snort. "Exactly so. Your Salukan friends are on their way. Reinforcements while we're a sitting target."

Melaethia's eyes widened. She stared at him, but he looked away, tired of her, unwilling to be kind.

"Dr. Beaulieu?" she said softly in appeal. "I do not understand."

Beaulieu put the approaching ship on the main viewscreen. *Theatrics*, thought Siggerson with a snort, as he knelt beneath the master station again and rummaged through his tool kit.

"She's gone, Siggerson," said Beaulieu's mocking voice. "You can come out again."

He probed a circuit and felt a jolt. At least one circuit wasn't completely dead. It was the first reassuring sign he'd had in hours.

"She looked scared. I'd better go talk to her," said Beaulieu.

"Stay," said Siggerson. "I've finally got something. A tiny nudge of response. Get down here and hold this probe. It could take hours to find that exact circuit again if my hand slips."

"What about that ship?"

"She'll either blow us to bits or she won't," said Siggerson, groping for a circuit loop with his free hand. "I can't worry about that now."

The sun had reached its scorching zenith by the time Dausal finally crept into sight. He wore goggles and a force belt. The latter's protective field shimmered gold about him. Kelly looked at the prong held in his sweating fist. No hope of penetrating the field with a knife. He shoved down the temptation to fire his pistol. Being caught in an energy web was not worth the chance to kill Dausal.

The Salukan hesitated a long while, thinking himself under cover. Finally, however, he came hobbling forth on his shortened leg. He went to where Phila hung suspended, and the quiet sound of his satisfied chuckle made rage run hot in Kelly's veins. He almost jumped from hiding then and there, but he held himself savagely in check.

"Kelly!" called Dausal in Glish. "You are nearby, I think. You are smart not to be caught here."

Kelly frowned as Dausal continued to stand beside Phila. Why didn't the force field attract the web? Was it attuned to specific frequencies? He noticed that Dausal held a percussion weapon, which would not attract the web.

"Kelly!" called Dausal. "The girl is not dead yet. Do you want her to live? Perhaps you will exchange yourself for her? I am told Earthers do such things."

Kelly closed his eyes to blink the sweat from them. He did not believe Dausal. He must not let himself believe. Yet he was glad that from this angle he could not see Phila's face.

"Her heart will give out soon. Perhaps she has another hour in the web. Perhaps she is stronger. Do you consider yourself a caring commander, Kelly?"

Still Kelly did not answer.

Dausal scowled, and gazed around. "Where are you?" he shouted. "Why do you not come out?"

"Why don't you give up?" said Kelly.

Dausal jerked, his head whipping from side to side as he sought the location of Kelly's voice. "Ah," he said, contorting his features into a smile. "So you will not leave the female."

"You've lost, Dausal. Your trap failed."

"Failed? I have her. Do you not see?" Dausal limped to the suspended wristband that Kelly had abandoned and pointed to it. "And I nearly had you. Now you cannot shoot me because the web will capture you. Give up this tiresome chase, Kelly. It is over. The ship will come soon, and I shall take the boy to his throne."

From overhead, something large and silver streaked through the sky. Dausal tilted back his head to gaze at it, and Kelly came scrambling from cover to tackle him. He and Dausal went rolling over and over in the dirt, Dausal's force field crackling between them. It kept Kelly from getting purchase upon Dausal, but Dausal had no such limitations. One of his hands, incredibly strong, closed upon Kelly's throat. The other struck Kelly in the face with his weapon.

The blow made Kelly's head ring. He fell sideways, fighting

to hang onto consciousness. Dausal reared up over him, aiming the pistol.

A shot rang out, and Kelly flinched involuntarily. But nothing struck his body. He realized belatedly that the sound had come from another angle, and that it was a plasma weapon. The web flashed.

"41!" he shouted, rolling to evade Dausal, who was also scrambling hastily for cover. "Watch out for the energy web!"

Kneeling, Dausal twisted his body and fired in the direction 41's shot had come from. 41 returned it, and the sound of the Maxell crashed heavily in the clearing. Its blast sliced off Dausal's gun hand at the wrist. Dausal screamed. There came the hot stench of burned flesh. The energy web crackled and flashed, but it seemed 41 was just beyond its range.

When the web's charge dissipated, there was only a weighty silence left. Dausal crouched upon the ground, clutching his severed arm with spasimodic jerks of pain. There was no blood. The bolt had seared off all the veins, arteries, and bleeders. The stump was cauterized, but he could die of shock. Beneath the goggles his face was already an ashen shade of yellow.

Kelly stood up cautiously. He went to the beacon and crushed it with his heel. 41 emerged from the rocks, and the child clung to his shoulder.

"You got here just in time," said Kelly with a grin. "Thanks."

41 nodded. His gaze went to Phila. "Is she dead?"

"I don't know," said Kelly. "We've got to find the transmitter and cut it off."

41 set the child on his feet. The boy swayed a moment then went to Dausal. Staying just out of reach, the child watched Dausal with stony eyes.

"We have not much time," said 41. "Beaulieu called. A Salukan ship has come into orbit."

"Then that was a shuttle overhead," said Kelly, frowning. "Have they spotted the *Sabre*?"

"She said yes. It has not hailed them."

"Damn. At least it hasn't shot them from the sky."

"It doesn't have to," said 41.

Ignoring that reminder of the problems besetting the damaged *Sabre*, Kelly squinted against the sun's glare. "This is all
the equipment I see. An energy web doesn't have much range,
so it must be close by."

They split up and began a quick, sytematic search through
the rubble of fallen building stones. When Kelly found it at
last, half hidden in a foundation niche, it was no bigger than his
hand. He'd never seen one this small and sophisticated before.
He ran his fingers over the black, featureless surface, but he
could not figure out how it worked.

41 stood listening. "I hear them coming."

Kelly dropped the transmitter and smashed it with a stone.

The web flashed in a brief but dazzling display of pyrotech-
nics, then failed. Phila fell to the ground.

Kelly reached her first. Gently he turned her onto her back,
smoothing her black hair from her face. Her skin was icy cold.
He caught only a tremor of her pulse. Her breathing was
shallow, jerky.

"Call the ship," he said, accepting his wristband which
41 picked up and handed to him. "We're teleporting out
now."

41 activated his comm and while he was speaking, Kelly
fetched the boy, who spat at him and dodged his grasp.

"Tut!" said 41 sharply. *"C'ai sale. Achei."*

The boy went to him at once, obeying the terse commands.

Kelly followed, studying 41 quizzically. "Looks like you've
started his training."

41 grunted. "Necessary. If he bites you, be sure to—"

The sound of the teleport interrupted him. But instead of
dematerializing, Kelly found himself watching a lone figure
appear before them.

Melaethia stood there, garbed in splendor with a beaded and
embroidered cloak that reached to the ground. When she
walked toward them, sunshine shimmered upon the rich hues
of crimson and silver. She carried a mask in her hand.

Astonished, Kelly stared. The boy started to run to her, but
41 gripped his shoulder. 41 knelt to put himself at eye level
with the boy and spoke to him in a low, urgent voice. Kelly met

Melaethia halfway, and when they stopped, facing each other, his face was hot with anger.

"What are you doing here? The Salukans—"

"The Salukans," interrupted a deep, unfamiliar voice in fluent Glish, "are here."

13

Though she walk veiled, honor thy mother all the days of her life. She has the strength of ten warriors and none can defeat her.

—from the Scroll of Solan

At the sound of that voice, Kelly whirled, weapon in hand, and saw a dozen Salukans clad in the blue tunics of a private army, all wearing force belts, all holding weapons aimed at him and 41. A man stood at their head, thin with razor-fine features and a narrow, shaven skull. The blue lines of a warrior were painted upon his cheeks. He wore a tunic richly embroidered in shades of dark blue and aubergine. The gold wire hilt of his House dagger reflected the sunlight brightly. In his slender hand he carried a rod of office.

Behind Kelly, Melaethia gasped aloud and raised her mask to cover her face.

Dausal struggled unsteadily to his feet. Clutching his wounded arm, he said, "Muetet, I have them for you—"

41 pushed him to his knees. "You have no one, *vasweem*," he said harshly.

Muetet flicked two fingers, and his soldiers ran to surround them. 41 was shoved away from Dausal, but no one offered assistance to the wounded man.

"Weapons," said one of the soldiers in Glish. "Down."

Kelly felt defeat like a bitter taste upon his tongue. To have fought so hard. To have finally ousted Dausal and his gang of cutthroats from control of the *Sabre*. To have been so close to getting away . . .

He looked at 41, and together he and 41 stepped between Melaethia and the Salukans.

"No," said Melaethia, and moved away from them.

The soldiers crowded in. "Weapons, down!"

Kelly frowned. If she rejected his protection, then he had to accept that. His gaze flickered at 41. He nodded. 41 dropped his pistol, and Kelly did the same. The guns were kicked out of reach, then the soldiers took their wristbands and hand-scanners too.

"Muetet," said Dausal, "you see what I have—"

One of the soldiers shoved his weapon muzzle into Dausal's face, and Dausal shut up with a low moan.

Muetet walked into the clearing with the slow grace of a man in a procession. When he came close enough, Kelly saw that he was pale skinned, paler than most Salukans, and had amber eyes. Kelly glanced at 41, then noticed that Muetet was also studying 41.

But Muetet's gaze came back to Kelly. "Your name."

"Commander Bryan Kelly."

"Kelly." Muetet's brows swept up. "I have acquaintance with this name. Admiral Kelly?"

Kelly could not quite repress a sigh, but he met Muetet's gaze firmly. "My father."

"An honorable warrior who has given the Empire much trouble. And I see before me a son who honors his father with bravery and courage. Are you firstborn?"

"No."

"Your brother runs the estates?"

In spite of his tension, Kelly almost smiled at the assumption. Muetet naturally dismissed the existence of any sisters. And the idea of Drew playing farmer was ludicrous. But Kelly did not intend to tell Muetet that his family owned no vast estates, for in Salukan eyes that would belittle Muetet's respect for the Kelly name. Right now, that respect was probably the only thing keeping Kelly and 41 alive.

"My brother," said Kelly, "is a commodore in the Alliance Fleet."

"A worthy family indeed." Muetet inclined his head, but Kelly did not return the salute. The Salukan kept his face impassive, his gaze narrow and hard. "This becomes no longer a matter of unknown troopers guarding that which we want recovered to us. You stand for much in the Alliance, Kelly. The damaged ship is in your command?"

"Yes."

Muetet's gaze went briefly to Phila, still lying unconscious on the ground, then returned to 41. "Your name."

"Operative 41."

Muetet's eyes narrowed slightly. Kelly wondered if he thought 41 was being insolent in giving him a number, but Muetet let it drop. "Half?" he asked.

41 hesitated for an instant. "Yes."

"Interesting." Muetet faced Kelly again. "I sent a force of Jostic fighters and three Salukans against you. Before me I see one of that number, and he is no longer whole. I see nothing of the ship I gave them."

"Their ship was destroyed," said Kelly, seeing no reason why Muetet shouldn't think his own squad had done the job. "Minlord Segatha and Chuteph are still alive. They are prisoners in our brig."

Muetet blinked in displeasure. "*Comme qu'sce thet?*" he said, half to himself. "How did this come about?"

Kelly smiled. "They aren't cowards. We removed the poison from their teeth."

"So." Muetet glared at Dausal a moment, then drew himself up. "I am the Nomarch Muetet ton Toth g Juvanne. I am head of the House of Toth. Through the maternal line of Dausal and the woman Melaethia, I have extended kinship to them since their father's House exists no longer. I claim the right to sponsor Melaethia's son, who is rightful Pharaon of the Empire. Step back from this matter, Earther. The Alliance has no claim here."

Kelly stiffened, aware of Melaethia hidden behind her mask, aware of the child, so small, so vulnerable. They all stood motionless in the bright sun, like chess pieces positioned upon an ancient stone playing board.

This is too big, whispered a small voice in his mind. *Not your decision to make*. Kelly knew Toth was a very powerful House in Salukan society. This man was essentially a head of state in his own right—powerful, wealthy, able to command his own army. The whole question of succession was vital to the Salukan Empire, a matter that needed to be discussed by diplomats. The realist in Kelly knew that eventually the little boy would be returned to the Empire. But not without a new treaty more favorable to the Alliance, necessitating many concessions from the Salukans.

However, the wrong move today could mean galactic war.

Kelly glanced again at the child, who had crouched and was now playing in the dust.

"Melaethia asked the Alliance for refuge," he said. "We uphold her rights. My orders are to protect her and her family. I do not retreat, sir."

Muetet smiled. "Words of honor, well spoken. But consider. You have been relieved of your weapons. Your ship is severely damaged. One shot from my ship will destroy her. I have no quarrel with you, Kelly. Unlike some, I do not kill idly; not even Earthers. You may go from this place freely, taking your crew and your ship. You know what is at stake. You know you have no claim in this matter."

"I know what's at stake," said Kelly, certain he had just started a war. "I do not retreat."

"Martyrdom does not become a warrior," said Muetet. "But if it is execution you wish, then—"

Melaethia stepped forward. "I will speak," she said in Saluk. Her husky, seductive voice rang out hard with purpose.

Muetet scowled. "This is not for women to interfere—"

"I am Masere!" she cried. "You will hear me now, Toth. You have offered kinship, but I have not accepted."

"I accepted!" shouted Dausal from where he knelt upon the ground. "Be silent—"

"No! You piece of cowardly dung, killer of our father, destroyer of his honor, betrayer!" She pulled off her mask and flung it in his face, tilting his goggles askew and scratching his cheek.

They all stared at her in shock, as much for her furious words as for the revelation of her face in public, before men.

"Cover yourself," murmured Muetet furiously. He gestured at his soldiers, and they averted their eyes. "Have you the madness?"

Melaethia's eyes shone. "I do not. Look at me, all of you! See the face of the favored concubine of Pharaon Nefir! See the face of the woman who killed him in vein-burn. The royal blood spilled by my hands reflects my courage. Though I may die for it when I am stoned by the twelve Houses, I have no shame. Unlike you, my brother the kuprat-eater."

Dausal staggered to his feet, ashen and enraged. "Fool! You brought down an Empire! You ruined my life, my career, my honor! You will die for it, and your son will be my puppet—"

Faster than thought, Muetet's dagger thunked into the soft part of Dausal's upper chest. With a soft, strangled cry, Dausal fell to the dirt. In the shocked silence afterwards, a soldier removed the dagger, cleaned it, and returned it to Muetet.

His eyes glittered as he sheathed the weapon. Melaethia's bravado crumpled. She stood there, no longer a queen, but only a young woman, her hands pressed to her mouth, her eyes wide upon the corpse that had been her brother.

The child rose to his feet and sniffed the air. Excited by the smell of blood, he ran toward Dausal's body, but Melaethia caught his arm and held him back. He yelled in frustration, but a sharp cuff from her quieted him. She picked him up and held him in her arms. Tears shone in her eyes.

Muetet picked up her mask and shook the dust from it. Wordlessly he handed it to her. She put it on, and in that instant Kelly knew for certain that she had made her decision.

"Is the boy yet named?" asked Muetet.

"No, Excellency," she replied in a low voice of submission.

Muetet's hand touched the boy's shaven head gently. He smiled into those small, fierce black eyes. "That is proper. It will be done soon. And training started."

Kelly frowned and stepped forward. "I'd like a word with Melaethia."

Muetet gave him a generous smile and waved the soldiers
back. He could afford to be indulgent now, thought Kelly
bitterly. Probably he was already building his palace in his
mind and gloating over the power that was coming his way.

41 took the boy from Melaethia's arms. Through the mask
only her eyes could be seen, and they still glistened with tears.

"Melaethia, are you sure?" asked Kelly urgently, keeping
his voice low. "You don't have to—"

"How can it be avoided?" she said bitterly, and now her
voice betrayed her fears. "Toth is a great House, as powerful
as Juvanne. To be claimed by them is to be protected. And
Muetet is known for his kindness. He may even keep me from
having to stand trial for Nefir's death."

Kindness. Kelly's gaze flicked briefly to Dausal, lying less
than two strides away.

"You'll never be free again," he said. From the corner of his
eye he saw 41 rubbing smudges of dirt from the boy's face with
an intense sort of tenderness that revealed a new side of his
friend. "Consider this, Melaethia. Do you really—"

"Better I go to them this way, of my own choice, than to be
handed over later by the Alliance," she said. "This increases
my worth. Otherwise, I am only chattel."

Kelly's frown deepened, but he knew she was right. "I'm
sorry," he said, unable to find a better way to express his
sympathy and regret. "We were supposed to help you, not
bring you back to this."

"I have had two years of freedom," she said. "I have seen
much. My son and I must give way to what destiny has brought
us. But my daughters will remain free." She gripped his wrist
with fingers that dug in. "Muetet's gloating has made him
forget them. Raise them, Kelly, in the free ways of Alliance
women. Let them become strong, able to think for themselves.
Let them have worth as individuals. Name them, Kelly. You
and 41 be their fathers and guardians." Her voice roughened
with tears. "Make my actions not be in vain. Teach them the
bravery of Arnaht, their grandfather who defied the Empire,
and help them to remember their mother, who surrendered to
it. The gods preserve you, Kelly."

"Melaethia—" he began, but she gave his wrist a warning shake and stepped back from him.

He saw Muetet watching and frowned, hating this. Melaethia had just begun to learn how to live life in a new way. To return to oppression, surveillance, and subjugation, to watch as her son was taken from her and raised by others . . . how could she agree like this?

But he knew, even as his mind asked the question. She had been born to it, raised to it. And lifelong conditioning to certain societal patterns was the hardest thing of all to escape. Melaethia couldn't, but she was right about her daughters. They had a chance.

He had just started to assimilate the burden of responsibility she had placed on his shoulders, when she turned to 41 and held out her hands.

41 gave the boy to her. His look was grave, his yellow eyes compassionate as he reached briefly beneath her mask and touched her face.

"*C'ai sale!*" called Muetet, irritated by that breach of etiquette. "Come, Melaethia!"

"Good-bye," she whispered to both of them, and walked away, her crimson cloak shimmering with brave color. Only then did Kelly recall that to Salukans red was the color of submission. The boy's face turned to watch Kelly and 41 over Melaethia's shoulder. His black eyes were stony, giving away no indication of whether he understood any of this.

"I think she is the bravest woman I have ever met," said Kelly quietly.

"Perhaps," said 41 cryptically, but before Kelly could ask what he meant, Muetet gave an order and their wristbands were returned to them.

The Salukans surrounded Melaethia and filed through the tall rocks at the edge of the clearing, heading back toward their shuttle. The ruins seemed suddenly quiet and empty. The alien air smelled sour. The sun beat down too brightly.

Kelly faced 41, who had gathered Phila in his arms, and said, "Let's go home."

On board the *Sabre*, Kelly stepped off the teleport platform, aware at once of the lingering smells of scorched metal and burned-out circuitry. Caesar, his arm still encased in a re-gen tube, operated the teleport. His grin of welcome faded when he saw Phila.

Jumping to his feet, he said anxiously, "She dead?"

Kelly shook his head. "No. 41, why don't you let me carry her to sickbay."

41 handed over his burden without a word. Kelly shifted her carefully in his arms, concerned by the stillness of her small face, aware of the vulnerable tilt of her head over his arm.

"What happened down there?" demanded Caesar, following them. "No, boss. We've got the lift working."

With relief Kelly swung back from the ladder well and entered the lift. 41 leaned against the wall, his face tight with exhaustion. Caesar looked at them both as the lift lurched upwards.

"Dausal set a trap. Did you get him? Where's the kid? Yusus, he didn't—"

"No," said Kelly. "Dausal didn't hurt him. Dausal is dead."

"Then where is the kid?" demanded Caesar, his green eyes widening. "What are you two looking like that for? You're giving me the creepilworts. If something's happened to him, Melly will have a fit."

Kelly frowned at him for a moment, then realization dawned. "Melaethia teleported down. Didn't you know that?"

"No. Beaulieu started to go down when you called, but then she called from the teleport bay and said you'd canceled the request. You saying she sent Melly down instead?"

"Looks that way," said Kelly grimly. He wanted to talk with Dr. Beaulieu.

But when they got to sickbay, Beaulieu took Phila off their hands and got busy. "Nasty jolt she took. Electrocution?"

"Energy web," said Kelly, watching in concern.

"Ah. I know how to deal with those effects," said Beaulieu with brisk satisfaction. She switched on a monitor panel. "Some very slow neural tracing for damage checks. She'll be groggy and disoriented when she wakes up. It will take time for that to wear off. Don't expect her help on the repair shifts, Commander. I'm keeping her in here."

"Yusus," muttered Caesar. "I forgot I'm supposed to be in engineering. Siggie will be having fits."

Kelly turned automatically with him. "How's it going?"

Caesar shook his head. "Not so good. I mean, we're being held together with spit and inertia right now. Siggie keeps muttering things about decaying orbits. But, boss, what happened to Mel and the kid?"

Beaulieu looked up sharply, her eyes probing. She drew in an audible breath and said, "What do you think, Samms? She went with the Salukans. Didn't she, Kelly?"

"Yes," said Kelly, and he couldn't keep the bitterness from his voice.

"Well, hell," said Caesar, scowling. "You mean we got our butts scorched for *nothing*? We damned near killed ourselves for her, and then she just goes off with them without so much as—"

"It's not like that, Caesar," said Beaulieu. "She made a very difficult choice, and there are two very frightened, very unhappy little girls in the next room who are already missing their mother."

"She left them too? What kind of—"

"What do you want, war?" broke in 41. He dropped heavily into a chair and rubbed his temples as though they hurt. "Kelly was set to take on the whole Empire. It was not worth it."

"Sure, and Commodore West is going to see it like that when we get home," said Caesar hotly. "*If* we get home—"

"Caesar," said Kelly, resting a hand on his shoulder. "She made a courageous decision, whether we agree with it or not. I think she's always known that she might have to go back one day."

"Yeah, and she murdered the old Pharaon and caused two years of civil war. They'll cut off her head for that."

"No, they won't," said 41. "She will be much honored as the Masere, Mother of Pharaon."

"Sure, and what do you know about it?" retorted Caesar. 41 shrugged.

"Headache, 41?" asked Beaulieu, eyeing him critically. She came at him with her scanner. "Yes, migraine spikes. Small wonder, with you insisting you were fit enough to go running around on a ground mission. And how much have you been walking on that leg?"

41 let her fuss over him, applying a drug patch and redressing his leg.

Caesar shook his head. "I'd better get back to work. Siggie's gonna love hearing about our candidate for mother of the year—"

"I did it!" yelled Siggerson, bursting into the sickbay and startling them all. Coolant was smeared in his hair, and his face and hands were filthy. He waved a circuit splicer enthusiastically. "I did it! The conversation generator is working!"

They all burst out talking in excitement, until Beaulieu finally shooed them from the treatment room and closed the door. "I've got patients in there. Do you mind?"

Siggerson danced her in a circle and grinned like a maniac. "It's working! It's working!" Abruptly he stopped dancing and faced Kelly. His face turned red, and Kelly wondered how long the knowledge of Siggerson's cowardice would hang between them. "Without the generator we couldn't utilize our light scoop. But now we've got all the power we need. No decaying orbit. No need for rescue. Of course we'll have to nurse her home gently. I can't get more than pulse power as shaky as the couplers are. But we'll make it."

"When? Six months from now?" asked Caesar.

Kelly frowned at him to be quiet, then faced Siggerson. He held out his hand, and after a moment of raw hesitation, Siggerson shook it.

"Good work, Mr. Siggerson," said Kelly, and smiled.

Siggerson smiled back, blinking rapidly.

A squawl over the sickbay comm broke up the moment. It was loud, hoarse, angry, and unmistakably Ouoji. They looked at each other.

"Beaulieu," said Siggerson, "is she awake?"

Another squawl shook the speaker. Beaulieu hastily reset the volume. "Obviously she is and sounds as grumpy as a . . ."

Letting her sentence trail off, Beaulieu vanished into the treatment room.

"Ouoji's okay," whispered Siggerson joyfully. He even slapped Caesar on the back. "She's okay!"

Caesar winked at Kelly and said in a grouchy voice, "Well, I bet next time she thinks twice about pulling a dumb stunt like that."

"Dumb!" said Siggerson in outrage. "I'll have you know that she knew precisely what she was doing. She extracted a laser probe from that illegal still you had stashed under the batteries and used it just where it—"

"My still," said Caesar. "Well, I guess if it hadn't been there Ouoji wouldn't have had a laser probe to use. And if she hadn't had a laser probe to use," he went on as Siggerson started to speak, "she wouldn't have been able to sabotage the power feed. Well, Siggerson? *Well*?"

Siggerson glared at him a long moment, then glanced at Kelly, who was watching in amused silence. "Yes, all right," he said with irritation.

"All right, what?" prodded Caesar.

"If not for your still, we would not be free now," said Siggerson grudgingly.

"You're welcome," said Caesar, and raised his brows expectantly at Kelly.

"Very well," said Kelly, giving in although he did his best not to smile. "No demerits."

Caesar grinned and gave Siggerson a nudge. "Come on. Let's get a drink before we go back to work."

"Bootleg or decent liquor?"

They went out before Kelly heard Caesar's reply.

Smiling, he shook his head and sat down beside 41, who had his head propped on his hand. Kelly's smile faded. "You took off the drug patch."

41 glanced at him. "Doesn't help."

"It might."

"No. Using the teachings of the Old Ones is always painful. It will fade soon."

Kelly frowned, uncertain of what he was talking about. "The Svetzin? Why should you be thinking about them?"

41 looked away with a shrug. "It does not matter. Kelly, Melaethia said that we are to raise her daughters. Do you intend to accept this guardianship?"

Startled, Kelly said, "I don't know. I hadn't thought about it yet. I suppose they should be turned over to child care experts and the Department of Displaced Children . . . but somehow I don't want to do that. I'd feel as though I let Melaethia down." He frowned. "How about you? You're in on this too."

"I have never been a father," said 41, his gaze remote as though his thoughts were far away. "I think we have been given a rare gift. I will not decline the honor of it."

Kelly laughed. "My God. I suppose I'll have to hire nannies. Or sent them to my mother. But the first one that bit her would—"

"I can teach them not to bite," said 41. He smiled shyly, and there was a suppressed eagerness in him that made Kelly realize how lonely he must be without any kind of a family of his own. "Which one will you choose?"

"Does it matter?"

"Yes. Which?"

Kelly thought, remembering the tough little body he had held in Melaethia's house, remembering how she squirmed and how she'd gazed deep into his eyes.

"The one with the purple eyes," he said.

"Ah, the youngest," 41 said, pleased. "She is best for you. Easier to train."

"Melaethia said we are to name them," said Kelly, still not quite certain he wanted to be a father. He had no immediate plans to settle down, and a child was always a complication. Maybe uncle would be easier to explain to his friends than dad. Maybe not. "Got any ideas?"

41's smile widened.

Beaulieu emerged from the treatment room and saw them sitting there together. "What are you grinning about?" she said suspiciously.

"We," said Kelly, deciding now was as good a time as any to drop the bombshell, "have just become fathers. Melaethia gave us the commission to raise her girls. I am taking little amethyst-eyes, and 41 gets her sister. How about Amethyst as a name?"

"She's not a pet or a gem," said Beaulieu acidly. "She's a Salukan child. And you—"

"I'll have to look up Salukan names," said Kelly. "Unless you know some, 41."

"Are you two serious about this?" said Beaulieu, lifting her brows. "You *are* serious about this. What about child care? What about education costs? What about a home life? Neither of you are equipped to—"

"It is not your decision," said 41 fiercely. "It is ours. I will pay for all that Naeitha requires." They stared at him, and he said with defiance, "Naeitha means Gift of Ru, or little sunbeam. Ru is the Salukan god of the sun."

"Yes, I know Salukan mythology," said Beaulieu. "Naeitha it is, then. But she's got to have your name too. Don't you think it's time you had a name of your own, 41?"

Kelly waited expectantly, but with a glare 41 got up and walked out, leaving Kelly and Beaulieu to stare at each other.

"41 in paternal mode," said Beaulieu. "That's a new one."

"He's very serious about it," said Kelly. "I guess I never realized he would ever want a family or children of his own."

Beaulieu looked thoughtful. "If he's serious, then he'll carry the job through. These children will be fine. It's their brother and Melaethia I'm worried about."

Kelly sighed. "We don't always win, do we, Doctor?"

"We can't. Odds are against that."

"She acted like a queen today. I hope they don't punish her. I hope they will be merciful."

"They could have shot us out of orbit and didn't," said Beaulieu. "They could have killed you and 41, and didn't. That's a lot of mercy right there."

"True. Maybe Melaethia will have a little influence over the new Pharaon. Maybe when he's grown he'll remember the stories of how he lived with Earthers for a short time. Maybe he'll be more receptive to ideas of peace."

"Big maybes, Kelly," said Beaulieu and shook her head. "I don't think we'd better count on that hope."

"Better hope than despair," he said and rose to his feet. "Speaking of despair, West is not going to be an easy man to face. I don't like failure. I don't like going home whipped."

"Do you feel whipped?" she asked.

He frowned. "No. I just feel that at some crucial moment

Melaethia took everything from my hands. I didn't expect her to have that kind of courage. It surprised me."

"It surprised me too. I hope she makes it."

Kelly nodded, but there was no more to say. He sighed. "I'd better start writing my report."

EPILOGUE

And the Empire is as a jeweled comb in the dark tresses of Night. He who rules the Empire is surely the Right Hand of God.
—Chronicles of the Second Dynasty

Four days into the journey to Gamael, Melaethia was summoned from her quarters. Masked and heavily robed, she followed the aide meekly and inclined her head to Muetet as she entered his sumptuous quarters.

Facing her were four other men, all scholars and advisers. Their faces looked grim and highly dissatisfied.

"Who," said Muetet, too angry to give her the courtesy of a greeting, "has dominated the boy? Who has imprinted him? What tampering has been done?"

Melaethia kept her lashes lowered, but behind the mask she grinned with a great leap of exhilaration. Even now, that last touch of 41's still tingled upon her cheek as a memento. It kept her courage from flagging. She also felt a rush of gratitude to her instructors in the Court of Women, who had taught her to conceal all things from her voice except pleasant, willing submission.

"This has not been done, Excellency," she said, her tones perfect beneath an artful touch of puzzlement. "The boy has witnessed much killing and fighting of late. It excited him, as is natural in one so young. Dausal separated him from me—"

"Dausal!" Muetet swore blackly. "That one dared too much. His domination is—"

"Forgive me, Excellency," she dared interrupt, "but I do not think my brother could dominate. He was most unstable, and domination takes longer than a few hours to achieve."

Except for one who knows advanced mental techniques, she thought. Techniques reserved usually for those in priestly roles; secrets hidden in temples within the great mountains or the deserts. She would never know how 41 came to have such knowledge, but she would always be grateful that he had reached her son in time.

The advisers conferred and nodded. Muetet's scowl deepened. "If Dausal caused little interference, then how does the boy resist us? Umhopec says he has already formed a personality, remarkable in one so young. And his resistance is very strong to any mind touch. You realize, Masere, that he must be taught allegiance to Toth quickly, before we return to the Defended City."

She thrilled by how automatically her title had fallen from Muetet's lips. Already she was accepted. Already her past was being forgotten. Already in this time of thwarted plans and frustration, Muetet was turning to her for advice. She would have some say in her son's education after all.

Umhopec scowled at her. "Has he naturally been domineering?"

She inclined modestly. "He is the eldest of three. Was it not natural that he control his two sisters?"

"Ah." Much conferring again. "A triple conception?"

"Yes," she said proudly, aware that the omen was great in her son's favor. "And Nefir's blood was strong."

"I think we must accept the boy's own strength of will," said Umhopec, as though he was somehow responsible for it.

Pompous lout, thought Melaethia.

Muetet rose to his feet and paced slowly about the room. "I am impressed," he said at last. "It changes some of our plans, but in the ultimate consideration, a strong Pharaon is better than a puppet. Our honor will be increased, and Toth's position will be strengthened. You have done well, Melaethia, in presenting us with a boy of this stature. We will educate him accordingly. Undominated. And he will name himself."

She inclined deeply, her heart singing with gladness and relief. They were safe now. And they would be treated well.

When she had been escorted back to her quarters, she slipped her hands up inside her mask to press her eyes until all the tears were gone. "Thank you, 41," she whispered too softly for the surveillance cams to record. Then she removed her mask and laid it upon her dressing table with quiet pride.